Hero's Adventure
The Hidden Crown

First Test Print Edition

Hero's Adventure

The Hidden Crown

Written by

Jim Ferguson

2025

Prologue

The Creation of Acklelend

In the beginning, God created the world. Yet, He did

not undertake this monumental task alone. To bring forth a realm of unparalleled beauty and boundless potential, He summoned the Nine Dragons of Existence—ancient, eternal beings born from the cosmic essence, each imbued with a sacred and unique purpose.

First to descend was the mighty Brown Dragon, whose enormous claws and powerful breath shaped the very bones of Acklelend from raw earth and unyielding stone. Mountains surged upward, piercing the heavens with majestic peaks, while deep valleys carved their way through the landscape, sheltering lush and fertile plains.

Following swiftly, the radiant Golden Dragon soared through the void, breathing radiant streams of light. It crafted the blazing sun, bathing the new world in warmth and illuminating the darkness. Countless stars were set adrift in the endless skies, glittering as beacons of hope and guidance, filling the universe with wonder and awe.

Then the Green Dragon gracefully swept across the barren land, breathing life into every crevice, every corner. From its breath sprang vibrant forests, expansive grasslands, and a myriad of blossoming plants, transforming the desolate landscape into a verdant paradise rich with flora and fauna.

The Blue Dragon followed, soaring elegantly above, its vast wings crafting the boundless skies. With deft strokes, it painted swirling clouds and summoned torrents of refreshing rain. Mighty rivers surged forth from mountain springs, serene lakes pooled in hidden valleys, and vast, untamed oceans embraced the lands, their waves whispering secrets of the deep.

Next came the Black Dragon, whispering softly, its breath creating the tranquil veil of night. Darkness spread gently across Acklelend, providing restful peace and sheltering creatures beneath a cloak of calm and quiet. In perfect, harmonious balance, the White Dragon spun delicate threads of time itself, orchestrating the perpetual dance of day and night.

The gentle Pink Dragon then approached, radiant and nurturing. With tender care, it cradled the delicate spark of life, bestowing it upon the creatures of Acklelend—the majestic beasts roaming the lands, graceful birds soaring the endless skies, shimmering fish darting through ocean currents.

Silently, thoughtfully, the Grey Dragon stepped forward, offering the solemn yet essential gift of death. A reminder of life's preciousness, mortality ensured balance and provided a profound, poignant beauty to existence's boundless joy.

Lastly, descending in fiery glory, the fierce Red Dragon crashed upon Acklelend's soil, gifting humanity the powerful yet perilous element of fire. Flames could offer warmth, cooking sustenance, and protection, but held within their essence the dangerous potential for devastating destruction.

United, the Nine Dragons shaped humanity from earth and magic, each bestowing upon them a divine gift:

The Golden Dragon granted mankind Consciousness - This gift is what separates humans from beasts: the burden of truth and the freedom of choice.

The Brown Dragon gave humanity strength and courage, a giving them the potential to face their fears and overcome them.

The Pink Dragon endowed humanity with Love, a profound and enduring bond capable of overcoming adversity.

The Blue Dragon imparted Friendship and Loyalty, forging unbreakable connections between souls.

The Green Dragon granted Knowledge and Healing, nurturing humanity's profound bond with nature.

The White Dragon offered Wisdom, a sacred understanding earned through experience and patience.

The Black Dragon presented the mysterious gift of Dreams, providing visions of the possible and impossible.

The Red Dragon instilled Passion, an intense and consuming force driving humans toward greatness or ruin.

The Grey Dragon revealed the enigmatic Afterlife, a hidden realm beyond mortal existence where souls could rest.

From God Himself came the final, wondrous gift— Creativity ...an inspiring spark that allowed humanity to transcend mere survival..., transforming them into innovators, dreamers, and artists.

Yet, unseen from the shadows, the cunning and jealous demon Zork crept forth. Envious of humanity's divine gifts, he whispered an insidious offer—Greed.

Greed corrupted humanity's blessings, transforming love into selfish desire, knowledge into dangerous ambition, and passion into destructive violence. Driven by greed, mankind became powerful yet arrogant, erecting mighty castles, crafting potent enchanted weapons, and inventing extraordinary magical machines. Among their greatest creations was the Treasures of the Nine Dragons and the Amnathoth Amulet, a magnificent golden necklace shaped as a dragon coiled around a glowing ruby, designed to locate and control the treasures and powers of the Nine Dragons.

But mysteriously, fate intervened, the treasures and the amulet were lost.

Freed from their enslavement and enraged by humanity's betrayal, the Dragons unleashed their fury upon mankind. They devastated great cities, toppled towers, and shattered the grand machines humans had so proudly built. Airships burned as they fell from the skies, and powerful empires crumbled into ruin and desolation.

Only the compassionate Pink Dragon, her heart filled with sorrow and unconditional love, pleaded with her brethren for mercy. Reluctantly, the Dragons agreed, yet their forgiveness was harsh and unforgiving. They spared humanity, ...but not without imposing terrible curses—eternal reminders of their prideful folly:

The Pink Dragon condemned humans to eternally broken hearts, endlessly searching for fulfillment.

The Black Dragon turned humanities nightmares to flesh, monstrous creatures lurking in darkness.

The Red Dragon instilled hate and violence, eternally driving humanity toward conflict.

The White Dragon cursed humanity with the inevitability of old age and harsh winters.

The Blue Dragon summoned violent storms and floods, relentless and unpredictable.

The Green Dragon made nature savage, beasts and plants turning perilously wild.

The Golden Dragon plagued humanity with relentless droughts, wilting crops and drying rivers.

The Grey Dragon unleashed virulent diseases upon the winds, threatening life itself.

And finally, the Brown Dragon reshaped some humans into strange new forms—elves, dwarves, orcs, goblins, and creatures stranger still, forever altering the tapestry of mankind.

Thus, human history fragmented into myth. Knowledge faded into whispers, kingdoms turned into legends, and humanity survived only as scattered remnants, clinging desperately to fading memories and whispered stories of their past.

Yet legends, like seeds buried deep within the earth, never truly die.

And some stories… are just beginning.

Part 1

The Hidden Crown

Chapter 1

The Boy from Golden Arrow

The mountain winds swept through Golden Arrow with

a whisper of cold, bending the high pines and rattling the dragon pens. Frost still clung to the wooden rails, and the scent of pine sap and distant smoke carried on the breeze. Morning light painted the valley in streaks of gold and silver, brushing the rooftops and icy peaks like a blessing from the Nine. As the village stirred, the quiet hum of voices and clattering tools echoed through the crisp air.

Sethery Bergan hoisted a sack of feed onto his shoulder, its rough burlap scraping his neck, and crossed the training yard, boots crunching over frozen dirt. Two unruly hatchlings—coal-black with flickers of orange along their spines—tugged at each other's tails near the enclosure. He sidestepped them with practiced ease, but not before one snapped at his boot and let out a sharp, indignant chirp.

The Lomeks were getting bigger. Meaner, too. Soon they'd be ready for their first ride. Someone would have to break them in—and more and more, it felt like that someone would be him.

"You're late," barked Master Rigg, a broad-chested man with a voice like falling stone and a permanent scowl etched into his weather-worn face.

"I'm early," Sethery shot back with a grin, adjusting the sack on his shoulder. "You're just impatient."

Rigg grunted, unimpressed. "Take that to Pen Four. The runt's not eating again."

Sethery nodded and headed toward the far pen, the chill stinging his cheeks. Inside, a small copper-colored Lomek crouched in the corner, its wings tucked tight and its glassy eyes watchful. Its scales shimmered with a reddish-black sheen, and it trembled faintly when he approached.

He crouched down slowly, careful not to make any sudden moves, and began speaking in a low, steady voice. "You're not so scary," he murmured. "Just stubborn."

The dragon flicked its tail but didn't hiss. A small victory. The kind that mattered.

Back at the house, the clang of hammer on metal rang out like a heartbeat. Lirien was at the forge again, sparks dancing around her like fireflies in a storm. Her apron was scorched, her dark hair tied back in a thick braid streaked with silver. She worked the blade with intense focus, sweat beading at her temples despite the cold.

She was the only smith in town who could forge weapons strong enough to withstand dragonfire—steel that shimmered with strange hues and held a resonance when struck. People whispered that she had once made finer things, rarer things. But she never said what or for whom.

Sethery dropped the empty sack by the door and leaned against the frame, watching her work in silence, the glow of the forge warming his face.

"You're old enough to take the ridge trail alone now," Lirien said without looking up. Her voice cut through the din with quiet certainty. "There's a delivery of silverleaf bark that needs fetching from Modo's Crossing."

He blinked, surprised. "That's a week's travel south there and back again. Isn't that—"

"Still safe, if you're careful," she said, interrupting him. Then she finally looked up, her eyes reflecting both the firelight and something unreadable. "And it's time you saw more of the world than this valley."

His heart fluttered. He'd dreamed of leaving—seen himself atop a dragon, crossing forests and ruins, finding lost things. But it always felt far away. Someday. Not now. Not today.

Still, he didn't argue. He couldn't. Not when her words struck something deep inside him.

That night, as the village quieted beneath the stars, Lirien packed him a satchel with dried meat, hard bread, flint, a waterskin, and a rolled parchment map marked in red ink. The scent of her forge still clung to her clothes.

9

Before he could ask why, she stepped toward the hearth and unhooked the shield that had hung there as long as he could remember. It was round, with a darkened rim, and in the center, set like a heart, was a pink stone that shimmered faintly, as if it pulsed with its own quiet rhythm.

"You'll take this too," she said. "It's yours now."

He stared at it, fingers tracing the metal edge, eyes drawn to the strange stone.

"Why?" he asked, his voice barely a whisper.

Lirien hesitated. For a moment, she seemed almost afraid. "Because there are things in this world older than you know, and some of them are waking up."

She kissed his forehead then, her lips warm against his cold skin. "Be careful, my son."

And before dawn, as a pale mist crept through the valley and the sky bloomed with pink and violet, Sethery Bergan stepped beyond the familiar paths of Golden Arrow for the first time in his life—shield on his back, pack on his shoulders, and a strange feeling stirring in his chest.

Something between fear and hope.

Something like destiny.

He had left the village before, for the high trails and the lower ridges—but never this far. Never past the shadow of the mountains. Never toward the world that had taken his father.

Romos Bergan, hero of Golden Arrow, had died when Seth was just nine. Killed in a skirmish by the Modo hill tribes. Seth remembered the flags, the silence, the look in his mother's eyes. He remembered feeling small and angry and full of questions no one wanted to answer.

Now, with the same shield his father once carried, he walked into that uncertain world.

Seth was halfway down the trail out of Golden Arrow when he heard it—a high, sharp screech from above.

He looked up just in time to see a flash of copper wings diving through the trees. The runt Lomek.

It swooped low and landed awkwardly on the trail ahead, claws scraping against rock. Its sides were heaving, and a leather strap hung loosely around its neck—one of the ones used for identifying hatchlings.

"What are you doing?" Seth asked, stepping forward slowly. "You're supposed to be in your pen."

The dragon let out a soft growl and cocked its head. Then, to Seth's surprise, it took a step closer and dropped something at his feet—a half-eaten squirrel.

"…Thanks?" he said, baffled.

The Lomek chirped and nudged his hand with its snout.

Seth looked around, but the trail was empty behind him. There'd be no getting this one back to the pens without a serious fight—and maybe, just maybe, it didn't want to go back. Maybe it had made a choice.

"Well," he muttered, "if you're gonna come with me, you need a name."

The dragon blinked its orange eyes at him.

Seth thought for a moment. "How about Ember?"

A small puff of smoke curled from the dragon's nostrils, as if in approval.

"Alright, Ember," he said, slinging his pack higher and nodding toward the forest trail ahead. "Let's see the world."

The two of them moved through the woods in tandem—boy and dragon. Seth kept to the old ridge path, winding through the dense forest that hugged the edge of the Impassable Mountains. Birds flitted overhead, and strange calls echoed from deep within the trees. Ember stayed close, alert, occasionally darting into the underbrush and returning with a curious treasure—an odd-shaped rock, a broken arrow, the torn flap of a weathered map.

By dusk on the second day, they made camp near the river. Seth sat with his back against a tree, eating dried meat while Ember snored softly nearby, tail curled around her small frame.

He pulled the shield from his back and studied it in the firelight. The pink stone at its center pulsed with a faint glow—slow and steady, like a heartbeat. Something about it felt… alive.

Seth reached out and touched the stone. Warmth spread up his arm, not heat, but something gentler—comforting, like the touch of his mother's hand. He knew the journey would only take a week, but already he missed her—and part of him still worried. What if something happened? What if he didn't come back? The thought of his father, lost to the hill tribes, stirred quietly in the back of his mind.

That night, as the stars shimmered above, Seth didn't sleep easily. There was a weight in the air, as if something unseen watched from the shadows beyond the trees. But Ember stirred only once, growling low, before settling again with a huff.

Whatever lay ahead, Seth knew this: the world was far bigger and far stranger than he had ever imagined.

And thanks to Ember, he was no longer alone.

The third morning brought clear skies and a crisp wind. The trail wound alongside a half-frozen stream and over ridges of granite. He was making good time.

That afternoon, not more than two hours from Modo's Crossing, the path narrowed through a thick patch of frost-wilted birch trees. That's when he heard it—a sharp rustle in the underbrush to his left. Then another. Too large for a rabbit. Too quiet for a deer.

He slowed.

"Let's move," he muttered, pulling his hood low.

They hadn't gone far when the trap was sprung.

A sharp whistle cut the air.

Three figures stepped onto the trail, blades drawn. Ragged cloaks, hungry eyes. Bandits.

"Hold it, kid," the tallest one said, raising a short sword. "Nice pack you've got. That shield too. Real fancy."

Seth took a step back, instinctively placing one hand on the pink-stoned shield across his back. Ember hissed, but it sounded more like a teakettle than anything intimidating.

The bandit leader sneered. "Cute pet. What's he gonna do, nibble my boots?"

Another one laughed.

Seth didn't reply.

Then, with a sudden flick, he tossed a pebble into the underbrush.

The bandits flinched, looking away for a heartbeat.

It was all he needed.

Seth ducked left and rolled behind a fallen log. Ember leapt from his shoulder and zipped into the underbrush like a dart. The bandits cursed, scattering to find him, but Seth moved fast. He unslung his shield, and as one bandit charged, he raised it.

The stone pulsed.

A soft pink light shimmered across its surface—and the attacker was thrown back as though hit by a force twice Seth's size. He hit a tree and dropped, groaning.

The second bandit hesitated. Seth met his eyes, breathing hard.

Ember reappeared suddenly—this time from above, leaping from a branch onto the back of the third bandit's head. The man flailed wildly as Ember screeched, biting at his ear and clawing for dear life.

"Get it off me!"

"Run!" the leader barked. "This ain't worth it!"

They vanished into the trees, Ember tumbling off and fluttering back to Seth's side.

Seth knelt and picked up the trembling little dragon, brushing dirt from her scales. "You okay?"

Ember gave a weak chirp, then sneezed—a tiny puff of smoke escaping her snout.

"You were amazing," Seth grinned. "You scared the pants off them."

He sat for a while, heart still pounding, watching the mist shift through the valley. "Well," he said, "I guess we're not in Golden Arrow anymore."

Chapter 2

Modo's Crossing

y end of the day, the trail widened again and flattened into a worn cobblestone road. The rooftops of Modo's Crossing appeared just past a crooked bend—simple homes, a modest trade post, and the flickering yellow glow of lanterns swinging in the breeze.

Seth entered the village quietly, eyes scanning the quiet square. A few locals bustled around—tying up goats, hauling sacks of grain, or setting out herbs to dry.

At the trade post, a round-bellied man looked up from a ledger. His eyes flicked to Ember, then to the shield on Seth's back.

"You from Golden Arrow?" the man asked.

Seth nodded. "Here for silverleaf bark. For Lirien Bergan."

"Well, that explains it. Thought she stopped sending folks down this way." The man ducked into the back room and returned with a tightly wrapped bundle, tied with red ribbon and wax sealed. "Fresh cut. Keep it dry."

Seth tucked the bundle safely into his pack. "Thank you."

The man leaned forward slightly. "You watch yourself out there. Been strange happenings lately. Creatures sniffing around where they shouldn't be. Not just bandits either."

Seth gave a polite nod, then turned back into the village.

The clouds had begun to gather, and thunder rolled somewhere in the distance. Rather than risk the trail in a storm, Seth found his way to a narrow wooden building marked with a carved sign of a snarling wolf's skull— The Modo Skull Inn.

Inside, the air was warm and smelled faintly of smoke, roasted root vegetables, and something sour on tap. A few townsfolk nursed drinks or played quiet rounds of Ranu—a popular local game involving colored wooden disks with different suits and numbers. Players bet on colors, trade for new pieces, and raise the pot as they reveal suits and numbers over multiple rounds. Ember perched on his shoulder, drawing a few curious stares, but no one bothered them.

Seth approached the bar and traded a few coins for a simple room and a bowl of stew. Ember sniffed at the meal with interest but curled up near the fire instead, clearly exhausted.

Later, alone in the modest upstairs room with its single bed and rattling window shutter, Seth sat on the edge of the mattress. He pulled the shield into his lap, its pink gem glowing faintly in the candlelight.

He had the silverleaf bark, the road home was clear—but his thoughts churned. About his mother. About the strange weight in the air. About the world waiting just beyond the next trail.

He slept lightly, dreams full of shifting shadows and wings.

Meanwhile, in Golden Arrow

Golden Arrow clung to the rocky cliffside like a stubborn root, its rooftops powdered in fresh snow. Wind whistled down from the Impassable Mountains, sharp and biting. Smoke rose from chimneys, and the clang of metal echoed from the town forge. In the square, archers loosed arrows at spinning straw targets, while Lomek wranglers led dragons through icy trails on tight leather reins.

But unease stirred beneath the surface.

Down near the hatchery, the air was thick with the scent of scorched herbs and molted scale. A newborn Lomek Dragon had been born too early—its wings thin and translucent, its cry high-pitched and unsettling.

"Not right," muttered Master Rigg, the elder wrangler, squinting at the little beast. "Something's shifting in the fire."

Belma, one of the younger handlers, ran her fingers gently along the dragon's spine. "It's like they feel something," she said. "Something they can't name."

Above them all, in her quiet cliffside home, Lirien sat cross-legged in front of a shallow silver bowl filled with water. She was motionless, eyes closed. The surface rippled on its own, though there was no breeze.

Then the bowl went still. Perfectly still.

A moment later, a cold pulse surged through the room—so faint most would have missed it. But not her.

Her eyes snapped open.

18

She stood, placing a hand on the cold stone wall. Her skin shimmered faintly—just for an instant—scales where there should be flesh, a soft gleam of ancient pink in her eyes.

Something… had changed.

A presence. Not here, but near. And not born of this time.

She couldn't name it, couldn't trace it, but in the deepest part of her soul—the part that remembered stars forming and the first dragons soaring—she knew:

A rift had opened. A force from the future now walked in the present.

"The time stone," she whispered. "Someone has found it."

She wrapped her shawl tighter and looked toward the southeast horizon.

"Sethery… come home quickly."

Down in the valley, near the mountain's shadow, a cloaked figure moved along the snow-dusted path. He paused briefly, looking up toward Golden Arrow. His staff—made from the twisted branch of a Lumnoop tree—hummed faintly with stolen warmth.

He grinned.

"The gate is ajar," he whispered. "Let's see what spills through."

Then he vanished into the falling snow.

19

Chapter 3

The Thief and the Shield

ethery Bergan sat on the edge of a wooden cart, the
scent of drying silverleaf bark rising from the bundle in his
satchel. The small village of Modo's Crossing bustled around
him—quietly, but not without life. Smoke curled from
chimneys, hens clucked lazily in the dirt paths, and a pair of
children played stick-ball near the blacksmith's forge.

He rolled his sore shoulders. The journey had taken three days
through uneven paths, dense forest, and, most notably, a brief
but fierce clash with bandits. They'd leapt out near Broken
Hollow Ridge, blades drawn and faces masked, thinking a lone
traveler would be easy prey. They were wrong.

His mother's shield—disguised in cloth and leather—had
protected him from the worst of the blows, its pink stone
briefly glowing when the final bandit struck. That flash had
startled them long enough for Seth to fight them off, one blade
to another, heart pounding in his ears.

Now, he rested in Modo's Crossing, seated just outside the
local tavern and inn: *The Modo Skull*. He sipped a watered-
down cider and watched the village go about its early morning
rhythm.

"Heading back to the mountains soon?" asked a voice beside
him.

He turned to see a stocky woman with dirt-stained hands and a woven reed basket full of herbs. Her gray braid hung over one shoulder.

"Yeah," Seth replied. "Just needed the bark. My village's healer's running low."

"Golden Arrow, right?" she nodded knowingly.

The woman gave an approving grunt and moved along. Seth glanced at the horizon. The sun had just begun its climb. He planned to leave shortly—three days back through the ridge and up into the Impassable Mountains.

But just as he stood to stretch his legs, he froze.

A ripple passed through the air. Barely a sound. More like a pressure—deep, unseen, and old.

It came not from the woods, nor from the village—but from somewhere else entirely. A sense of time shifting, like a thread being pulled taut across centuries.

A presence. Evil. Patient. Not born of this time.

Seth gripped the leather wrapping of the shield strapped to his pack. It pulsed faintly, warm against his palm.

He didn't know what it meant, but his mother's words echoed in his mind:

"The world is older than it admits. Some things lost may be waiting to be found."

And some things found, he thought, are better off lost.

21

In the early light, the air buzzed with noise—merchants barking out deals, goats braying in the street, boots slapping against the cobbled road. Seth adjusted the satchel at his side, tucking the Silverleaf Bark deeper inside as he made his way through the crowded market square. The people here were loud, fast, and very good at bumping into you without apologizing.

He wasn't used to cities.

Perched on his shoulder, Ember clung like a velvet shadow—her small claws dug lightly into his cloak, and her tail wrapped around the back of his neck. She blinked slowly, golden slit-pupiled eyes scanning everything with suspicious curiosity. Her scales shimmered a deep reddish black, like glowing embers under ash.

Seth reached up and gently scratched under her chin. "You doing okay, girl?"

She purred—a low, throaty rumble—and licked his ear with a tongue like warm velvet.

A girl bumped into him—barely more than a brush of her shoulder—and muttered an "Oops" before melting into the crowd. She had a hood drawn low, and something about her gait struck Seth as odd. Too quick.

It took him several steps to notice the weight on his back had shifted.

His mother's shield—the pink-stoned shield—was gone.

Seth spun, heart lurching. Ember flared her wings and hissed, her eyes narrowing in the direction the girl had gone. She launched from his shoulder and darted into the air, weaving above the heads of the crowd like a crimson streak.

"There!" he shouted, shoving through the people. Ember circled once above a side alley and let out a sharp trill before diving out of sight.

He pushed past a fruit stand, knocking over a basket of apples as the vendor shouted behind him, and turned into the alley. Empty. No trace of the girl. No shield. Ember landed lightly on a windowsill, sniffing the air with little snorts, then gave a low, annoyed growl.

"I know," Seth muttered, heart pounding. "She's fast."

For the next few hours, Seth scoured the city—asking vendors, peering into windows, doubling back through alleyways. Ember rode on his shoulder again, tail twitching with frustration, occasionally leaping off to chase a scent or peek down a chimney.

A young stable boy claimed to see someone matching the description heading toward the edge of town, near the broken aqueduct. That's where they went.

There, nestled in the shadows of the crumbling stone, he found her.

As he stepped into the shadows beneath the broken aqueduct, his boots crunching against old gravel, he spotted her—lounging like she owned the place, legs crossed, chewing on the last bite of a green apple. His shield rested beside her, propped casually like a tray. Ember perched silently on a branch above, tail coiled tight and wings half-folded, watching.

"You should learn to tighten your straps," she said, mouth half-full, not even looking up, the girl said before Seth could speak.

"You should learn not to steal," he snapped.

She grinned and tossed the apple core over her shoulder. "Then we'd never have met."

Ember dropped soundlessly from the branch and landed beside Seth, puffing a small cloud of smoke as she stared at the girl.

She finally looked up. Bright eyes. A crooked smile. Younger than he'd expected, but sharp. "I don't steal. I rearrange ownership."

"You rearranged my family heirloom."

She stood and dusted her cloak off with an exaggerated flourish. Ember hissed softly. The girl raised an eyebrow but didn't flinch.

"Well, you left it dangling like a prize hog at a Fergo feast. I assumed you didn't want it anymore."

"It was strapped to my back!"

"A loose strap is practically an invitation. I thought maybe it was some strange Zarnoth custom—leave an enchanted shield out for strangers and hope for new friends."

Seth scowled, stepping closer. Ember growled.

"You know it's enchanted?"

She tilted her head. "Please. I can sniff magic from a mile off. That pink stone? Practically humming."

Seth clenched his fists. "Give it back."

The girl rolled her eyes. "Relax, country boy. I wasn't gonna sell it. Just wanted to see who'd come chasing after it."

He blinked. "You wanted to be chased?"

"Well, not just anyone, obviously. But you? You look interesting."

"Interesting?" he echoed.

She picked up the shield and spun it toward him like a coin across a tavern table. He caught it with a grunt. Ember leapt up to perch on the rim, her tail flicking across the pink gem protectively.

"Don't get too flattered," She added, smirking. "Your tracking skills are average. I left like five clues."

"I followed you through a city I've never been in before," he shot back.

"Exactly. Average." She grinned.

Seth stared at her, trying to decide whether he should still be angry. Ember nudged his cheek with her snout, a quiet reassurance. He exhaled.

"I'm Ro," she said, sticking out a hand.

"You steal from me and now you want to shake hands?"

"I didn't steal. I borrowed. And I gave it back." She wiggled her fingers. "Come on. Don't be dramatic."

Seth hesitated… then shook it. Ember gave a low grunt, clearly still not impressed.

"Nice grip," Ro said. "You're stronger than you look. Still kinda soft, though. Golden Arrow, right?"

He narrowed his eyes. "How do you know that?"

She winked. "I have a talent for knowing things I shouldn't."

They walked side by side through the outer edge of Modo's Crossing, the dirt path lined with leaning huts of driftwood and bundled reeds. Nets hung between poles like sleepy flags, drying in the breeze. Just beyond the village, the wide River Molden curled like a shining snake through the marshy lowlands.

In the shallows, fishermen rode tall, elegant Gorla Storks— massive birds with long, glinting beaks and pale violet feathers. The storks waded slowly, dipping their heads beneath the water's surface and coming up with wriggling silverfin clamped between their serrated beaks.

Ember rode draped over Seth's shoulders again, her eyes half-lidded, tail twitching lazily. She made a soft chirping sound every time one of the storks caught a fish.

Ro kept a casual pace, her boots squelching now and then in the damp earth. "Nice town. Smells like boiled socks and sadness."

"Stop following me," Seth muttered, eyeing a merchant cart stacked high with river clams steaming over a firepit.

"I'm not following. I'm walking. This road just happens to be going the same you are," Ro replied with a shrug.

"Oh? And where's that?"

She paused to grab a ripe red fruit from a passing basket cart, flipping a copper to the vendor. "Wherever there's trouble. Or lunch. Or both."

Seth rolled his eyes. "I don't need company."

"I'm not company. I'm local flavor."

He stopped walking and faced her. Ember sat up straighter, watching Ro with a slow blink.

Behind them, one of the Gorla Storks gave a low, throaty honk as its rider tossed a fish into a woven creel. The town buzzed around them—soft barter calls, children chasing frogs near the riverbank, and the flap of stork wings as one took to the sky with surprising grace.

"Seriously," Seth said, lowering his voice. "Why are you tagging along?"

Ro bit into her fruit and shrugged. "I have a feeling about you. That shield isn't ordinary, and you're not just some errand boy off gathering bark. I'm curious."

"Well, stop being curious. You already stole from me once. I don't trust you."

She grinned. "Smart. Trust is just a trap people build for themselves."

"You're really making this hard."

"Listen, hero," she said, hopping onto a low wall made of piled stones, balancing as she walked along its edge. Behind her, tall rivergrass swayed in the breeze, and the thick scent of moss and woodsmoke filled the air. "You don't trust me? Fine. I wouldn't trust me either. But I can be useful. I know these parts. I've seen things that would boil your blood. And I've survived them."

Seth narrowed his eyes. Ember licked his cheek once and gave a soft, warbling chirp.

That made up his mind.

"Fine," he muttered. "But if you try anything—"

"You'll what?" she teased. "Shield me to death?"

"I'll do something."

"Ooooh. Vague threats. Love it."

He picked up his pace, grumbling, "This was a mistake."

Behind him, Ro dropped off the wall and sauntered after him.

"Mistake or not, you're stuck with me now. Try to keep up, golden boy."

Ember let out a low chirp that sounded suspiciously like a chuckle and nestled deeper into the crook of Seth's neck, her warm weight a quiet comfort.

The path northward from Modo's Crossing followed the winding River Molden, slicing through the edge of the Whispering Thickets. The riverbanks shimmered with wet moss, and towering roots hugged the trail like skeletal fingers. Strange birds circled overhead, and stork-riders glided above the water—fishermen balanced on saddles strapped to massive, storks. As the storks dove with uncanny precision, plucking silverfin from the depths and flinging them back to their riders in a well-practiced rhythm.

Ro tilted her head, watching the aerial ballet. "You ever ridden one of those?"

"No," Seth replied, resting a hand on Ember's warm flank as she walked beside him, silent and alert. "They say the storks only bond with riverborn folk. The rest end up face-first in the water."

Ro grinned. "Sounds like a challenge."

Ember snorted softly, as if unimpressed by the idea, her wings slightly twitching with every splash and call from above.

Their path curved into thicker woods, where the light dimmed beneath twisted branches and lichen-draped trees. The air turned cooler, heavier. Ember's scales, usually warm to the touch, felt suddenly tense beneath Seth's hand.

Then Ro froze. "Something's wrong."

Seth halted. Ember's golden eyes narrowed, nostrils flaring.

The forest was too quiet. No birdsong. No river sounds. Just breath. Heartbeats. Tension.

A low rustle to the left.

From between two mossy stones stepped a creature just about three feet tall.

A ball of fur with eyes and a mouth—no neck, no nose, just thick, matted green hair and a wide, jagged grin.
Its limbs were long and thin—scaled like a bird's, with sharp yellowish talons that clicked softly on a fallen branch.

A Lopkin.

Ro swore under her breath. "These things don't come this close to towns."

29

"They don't," Seth said, stepping closer to Ember, hand on the hilt of his dagger. "They live deep in the Dark Forest. This far north…"

The Lopkin crept forward, low to the ground, moving with an eerie calm, its glowing green **eyes** locked on them.
And it didn't blink.

"You… not sssafe…" it croaked, its voice ragged and dry. "Path twistsss… yesss… mm… I sssmell it…"

Ro stepped forward. "What do you want?"

It ignored her, lifting its face toward Ember.

"Fire… memory… old blood… yesss…"

Ember growled—low and guttural—her wings flexing once. The sound rippled through the trees like a warning.

The Lopkin didn't flinch. Instead, it hunched forward, sniffing the air again.

"One breaksss. One betraysss. Mmm… not end… but bend…"

Seth whispered, "That's a green one. It can control plants— bind you before you even move."

"And it's talking to us," Ro muttered, uneased. "They don't talk to warriors. They don't talk to anyone. Not unless…"

"Unless they think you're magical," Seth finished.

The Lopkin crouched, dragging a jagged sigil into the dirt. Nearby vines twitched—restless, like snakes sensing prey.

"Fire not yersss… water not yersss… time sssplitsss… ssso much pain…"

Its gaze shifted between Ro, Seth, and Ember. "You dream of clawsss and fire… you run toward it…"

Ember stepped forward, placing herself between Seth and the creature. Her chest glowed faintly pink—barely visible, but enough to reflect in the Lopkin's eye.

It flinched.

"Time will know… sssecretsss show…"

Then—swift as a blink—its claws plunged into the soil.

A wall of brambles exploded upward, thorns curling like spears. Ro rushed over quickly, pushing Seth out of the way as vines whipped toward him—but halted inches away, from her. Almost like they feared her.

By the time Seth hacked his way through the brambles, dagger flashing, the creature was gone.

Only a faint ring of mushrooms remained, pulsing softly with green light.

Ro spat. "I hate forest magic."

"You and me both."

Ember huffed and shook out her wings, the bramble wall already withering behind her.

Ro glanced sideways at Seth. "So… 'one breaks, one betrays'… That supposed to be us?"

"I don't know," Seth said. "But I'm not planning on either."

Ro gave a half-smile. "Same here. But don't think for a second I'm not watching your back. Just in case."

He chuckled. "Thanks… I think."

They moved on, deeper into the woods, Ember walking just ahead—her wings low, tail swaying, eyes scanning every shadow. The forest was quiet again, but the air still held the taste of prophecy.

Golden Arrow lay ahead.

And far behind, beneath vine and root, a Lopkin watched with its green eyes… and remembered.

By nightfall, they found a quiet patch just off the winding river road—close enough to hear the steady flow of water and the rhythmic splashes of the giant river storks as they dove, their long beaks flashing in the moonlight. The clearing was soft with pine needles and moss, and the fire crackled with a low, comforting hiss.

Ro sat with her back against a rock, flipping a dagger between her fingers with casual precision. Seth crouched beside the fire, stirring a modest pot of riverweed stew, nose wrinkled as he gave it another cautious sniff.

Nestled beside his pack was Ember, the tiny copper-scaled Lomek dragon no larger than a curled-up housecat. Her eyes, bright and alert, tracked the flickering firelight while her stubby wings twitched in her sleep. She let out a soft chirp and puffed a little smoke ring that fizzled into the air.

"She's so small," Ro said, nodding at Ember.

"She hasn't grown much," Seth replied. "She eats, she naps, she chews things, and then she eats again."

Ro grinned. "Sounds like you two were meant for each other."

"I raised her before I left Golden Arrow. She was the smallest in the hatchery—sickly, ignored. The others wouldn't go near her. I couldn't just leave her behind."

"Must've had a soft spot for runts," Ro said, smirking. "Or maybe you just wanted to impress the girls with a pet dragon."

Seth gave her a sidelong glance. "She's not a pet."

Ro raised her hands in mock surrender. "Okay, okay. Faithful companion."

He smiled despite himself, gently running a hand down Ember's back. Her scales shimmered faintly, a dull copper hue that caught the firelight like aged metal. She let out a soft, pleased trill.

Ro glanced up at the darkening sky. "You mountain folks live different lives. Dragons, enchanted trees, legends hiding behind every rock."

Seth turned back to the fire. "And you don't?"

"I've seen a few legends," she said, resting her chin on her knees. "Usually while stealing coin purses in Zarnoth."

He gave a slight grin. "You're very open about being a thief."

"I'm not. I'm just being polite."

Seth shook his head, but he was starting to enjoy their banter. Still, there was a guardedness in his voice when he asked, "So why are you really coming with me?"

Ro didn't answer right away. She watched the flames dance, shadows flickering across her face.

"Let's just say I have a nose for interesting things," she said. "And that shield of yours? Very interesting."

Seth didn't reply, but the way he watched her said enough. Trust would take time—if it ever came at all.

Ember stretched in her sleep, let out a tiny hiccup, and a puff of smoke spiraled toward the stars.

"You're not like most people I've met," Ro murmured.

"Is that a good thing?"

"It's definitely a thing."

A gentle breeze rustled the trees, and somewhere beyond the river, the storks called out with strange, echoing cries. The fire popped, the stew bubbled low, and the tiny Lomek dragon let out another soft chirp as the two travelers sat in quiet tension, bound by coincidence… or something more.

Chapter 4

The Return to Golden Arrow

he journey back to Golden Arrow was uneventful, save for the strange encounter with the Lopkin that had unsettled them both. The creature's cryptic warning had stayed with Seth, though it was hard to make sense of the words it had spoken. His mother's voice echoed in his mind, reminding him of things she had said about the world being older and more complicated than most understood. But for now, it seemed that the wild woods and the road ahead were all that mattered.

Seth had left Golden Arrow with a sense of uncertainty, unsure of what lay beyond the familiar valley. Now, as he approached the town's gates once again, a strange calm settled over him. The mountains loomed in the distance, their snow-capped peaks familiar and solid, like old friends returning after a long absence.

The village looked much the same as he had left it. The smoke still rose from chimneys, the clang of the smith's hammer still rang from the forge, and the scent of pine and woodsmoke still filled the crisp air. It felt good to be back.

Seth had brought Ro along, despite the awkwardness of the situation. She wasn't a permanent fixture in his life—not yet, anyway—but there was something about her curiosity, her boldness, that kept him from sending her away. Besides, she'd proven useful on the journey, even if her teasing and unpredictable nature made him wary.

Ro had taken to the village with the same ease she had shown in the larger cities. She was quick to blend into the background, observing quietly, making comments here and there that piqued Seth's interest. As they crossed the wooden bridge that led to his family's home, he could see the quiet curiosity in her eyes.

"Well," Ro said, glancing around as they walked through the village, "this place looks... familiar. Comfortable, even."

Seth couldn't help but laugh. "It's as ordinary as it gets," he said. "People here don't go looking for trouble. They make their lives as simple as they can."

As they approached the stone house at the edge of the village, where his mother's forge stood tall against the surrounding trees, Seth felt a rush of warmth. His mother, Lirien, would be inside, busy at the anvil, her dark hair pulled back into a braid that shimmered with silver streaks. The faint hum of magic in the air made it feel like the whole house was alive with energy.

Ro raised an eyebrow as they approached the door. "This is home?" she asked, her tone just the right mix of intrigue and surprise.

Seth nodded. "Yeah. It's not much, but it's ours."

He opened the door to the warmth of the hearth and the soft glow of the forge. The clinking of metal echoed from the far side of the room where Lirien was hard at work, hammering at a piece of glowing iron. Her focus was absolute, her movements practiced and sure.

"Mother," Seth called, stepping into the room with Ro just behind him.

Lirien looked up, a smile crossing her face when she saw Seth. "Back so soon?" she asked, wiping the sweat from her brow. "Did you manage to get the silverleaf bark?"

Seth nodded, reaching into his pack to pull out the wrapped bundle. "Got it, and it's fresh." He set it down on the workbench, where she immediately began unwrapping it.

"And you brought company," she noted, glancing over at Ro with a small, welcoming smile. "Who's this?"

Ro stepped forward, offering a hand, her usual mischievous grin still firmly in place. "Ro. I'm a traveling... friend of Seth's. Pleased to meet you, ma'am."

Lirien eyed the young woman, her expression unreadable. After a moment's pause, she took Ro's hand. "Lirien Bergan," she replied simply, her grip firm but measured.

Seth gave his mother a small nod, still unsure how to break the silence, and he stepped inside. "It's good to be home," he said quietly, allowing the warmth of the house to settle around him. Ember fluttered down to land on the hearth, curling up as the fire crackled.

Lirien didn't say anything for a moment. She turned her gaze to Ro, then back to Seth. Finally, with a soft sigh, she motioned for them both to sit at the long wooden table.

"I think it's time you learned some things, Seth. Things you weren't ready to hear before," she said, her voice heavy with something ancient and sorrowful.

Seth's heart skipped. He could feel the weight of her words, and a deep unease settled in his chest. Ro, too, seemed to sense the change in the air, her brow furrowing slightly as she sat down next to Seth, keeping her eyes on his mother.

Lirien's gaze turned inward, and for a moment, Seth could see something flicker in her eyes—something ancient, almost otherworldly. She placed her hands on the table, her fingers slowly tracing the worn wood.

"You already know that I am not just a simple blacksmith," she began. "But you do not yet know the full truth."

Seth leaned forward, his curiosity piqued, but it was Ro who spoke first.

"You're not just a blacksmith?" Ro asked with a raised eyebrow, glancing between Seth and his mother. "Then what are you?"

Lirien hesitated for a moment before speaking again, her voice barely above a whisper. "You know the stories. The Nine Treasures of the Dragons—everyone has. They're told as legends, bedtime tales to make children dream and adults scoff."

She looked up, her gaze sharp. "But they're real. I know, because I am one of the Nine Dragons of Existence. In human form."

The words hung in the air like an invisible weight. Seth's breath caught in his throat as he stared at her, disbelief and shock flashing across his face. Ro remained still, her gaze fixed on Lirien, but there was a certain understanding in her eyes, a recognition that she kept carefully veiled.

Lirien went on, her tone more somber. "There are nine of us, born at the dawn of time. Each of us was reflected in one of the Nine Treasures—artifacts of immense power, each forged by mortal hands with a gem that drew its strength from one of us. And one of those treasures is the shield you carry."

She leaned back, eyes distant.

"The Nine Treasures," she said slowly, "They were created by ancient mages and smiths—mortals who sought to harness the essence of the Nine. Each artifact was a channel to our elemental power, not a gift from dragons, but a mortal-made link to us.

"They were not made lightly. Entire lifetimes were spent forging them. Some were born in fire, others in death. The makers paid dearly for their creation. But in the end, they succeeded. And the world was never the same."

She looked up, her gaze sharp and unwavering. "If someone were to claim all nine—if they were to bring them together— they would hold the power of creation itself. They could unmake the world as it is... or reshape it entirely to their will. That is why they must never fall into the wrong hands."

"Mine was the Shield of Compassion—forged in rose gold with a pink gem that pulses with empathy. It protects, but it also reveals the hearts of those nearby. You've felt it, haven't you?"

Seth gave a small nod.

"You've heard the names in stories," Lirien said. "But stories don't tell the truth. Let me tell you what they really are."

She took a breath and began to list them, one by one, her voice quiet but deliberate:

"The Shield of Compassion, now in your possession, forged in rose gold with a pulsing pink gem. It protects—and reveals the hearts of those nearby.

"The Aquarian Crown—a silver circlet glimmering like seafoam, with a teardrop blue gem. It grants dominion over water and sky, and strengthens loyalty among companions.

"The Gauntlets of Verdance—shaped from emerald stone beneath the oldest tree, bearing a glowing green gem. They heal and command vegetation.

"The Stonebreaker Hammer—made in the depths before dwarves walked Acklelend. With its rich brown gem, it shatters stone and bends the earth.

"The Flameforged Sword—born of the Red Dragon's fire. A flickering ruby in its hilt feeds its fury. Its edge burns with wrath.

"The Cloak of Nightmares—stitched from shadow, soaked in fear, bearing a black gem that shimmers like smoke. It commands illusions and gives shape to terror."

Ro let out a low breath, arms crossed. "Great. I had nightmares about that one when I was little. Thought it was just a story to scare kids into behaving." She glanced between Lirien and Seth. "Thanks for confirming it's real. I'll be sleeping *so* well tonight."

"The Hourglass of Echoed Time—crafted in grief, held by a pale white gem. Its sands can be persuaded to run forward or backward.

"The Soul Lantern—lit from the breath of a dying god. The gray gem at its core guides lost spirits—or calls them back.

"And the last: the Sunfang Dagger—a radiant golden blade with a sunburst gem. It steals life, reveals truth, and pierces even the deepest lies. Not just a weapon. A judgment."

Seth swallowed hard, his fingers tightening around the handle of the shield, feeling the faint pulse of the pink stone against his palm. He had always known the shield was special, but this? This was beyond anything he had ever imagined.

"I never meant for you to find out like this, Seth," Lirien continued, her voice trembling slightly. "But the time has come. You are not just a boy from Golden Arrow. You are part of something much larger."

Seth opened his mouth to ask more questions, but Ro spoke up before he could.

"I didn't know you were one of the Nine Dragons, but I knew this shield had something to do with the treasures," she said, her fingers gently tapping the gold dragon necklace at her throat. It was a beautiful, ornate piece, the ruby glinting under the firelight. "This," she continued, "is the Amnathoth Amulet. It was made to find the Nine Treasures of the Dragons. That's how I found you."

Seth's head whipped toward Ro. "You've been looking for the treasures?" he asked, his voice low.

Ro met his gaze, her expression unreadable. "I've been following the clues for a while. The amulet guides me. It's how I came to you. I wasn't sure what I'd find, but I had to follow the path."

The air in the room grew heavy with the weight of secrets, the flickering fire casting strange shadows on the walls. Seth's mind raced with the sudden flood of information. His mother, one of the Nine Dragons of Existence. The shield he had carried for as long as he could remember, now revealed as one of the Nine Treasures. Ro, a mysterious traveler with a magical amulet that led her to him.

And yet, despite the enormity of it all, there was a sense of clarity beginning to form within him. The pieces were falling into place, one by one.

"So... this shield," Seth said slowly, looking at his mother, "it's one of the treasures. Does that mean... I'm supposed to find the others?"

Lirien nodded, her gaze soft but resolute. "Yes. But it's not just about the treasures, Seth. It's about what they represent—what they can do. There are others who will seek them for their own purposes."

Seth looked down at the shield, then back at his mother, his resolve slowly building. "I don't know what all of this means yet, but I want to understand. I need to know."

Lirien gave him a faint smile, her eyes glistening with a mixture of pride and sadness. "I knew you would, eventually. But be careful, Seth. The path you walk is fraught with dangers, and not just from those who would seek the treasures. The past has a way of catching up with us."

Seth felt a chill run down his spine, but he nodded, determined. "I'll be ready."

Ro leaned back in her chair, eyeing Seth and his mother with quiet interest. "So, what now? I'm guessing there's a plan?"

Lirien looked to Seth, then back to Ro. "For now, you stay here. Rest. Tomorrow we begin to prepare. The journey will be long, and the road ahead is uncertain."

Seth nodded, still absorbing everything. He had come home seeking nothing more than to deliver a simple errand—and now, his life had changed forever.

And as he looked at the amulet around Ro's neck, and the strange glow of the pink stone in his own shield, he realized that whatever lay ahead, it would be nothing like the world he had known before.

The adventure had only just begun.

Chapter 5

A Rift in Time

he morning had arrived quickly, and Seth and Ro found themselves preparing for the journey ahead. Their packs were light but filled with the essentials, the promise of an uncertain future hanging between them like a dense fog. As they discussed their next steps, Lirien sat quietly by the hearth, her brow furrowed with the burden of what needed to be done.

Before they left, Seth's mother gathered them both, her expression serious. She had waited for this moment—one she had known would come, though not so soon. Something had already begun, something Seth had no idea was unfolding.

"The shield you carry, Seth," she began, her voice steady but threaded with urgency, "is the first of the Nine Treasures and it will help you on your journey."

Seth nodded, his hand resting on the shield's pink stone, the gentle pulse of magic still humming faintly.

"But there's something else you must know," Lirien continued, her gaze distant, as if seeing far beyond the room. "Something happened while you were away in Modo's Crossing. Something that disturbed the flow of time."

She paused, letting the words settle.

Seth exchanged a glance with Ro, who said nothing, though her stance had shifted—alert, cautious.

Lirien rose and moved to the window, her figure outlined in the pale morning light. "I was meditating, trying to feel the presence of the other dragons. That's when it happened."

She turned back toward them, her eyes faintly glowing.

"I sat before a silver bowl filled with water. The surface rippled though the air was still. Then the bowl went silent—and I felt it. A cold pulse. Subtle, but ancient. My skin shimmered— briefly scaled—glowing pink."

Seth stepped forward. "What does that mean? What did you feel?"

"The presence wasn't from here. Not from now. It came from beyond time."

Her voice was softer now, caught in memory. "It was the Time Stone, Seth. It's been found. And its awakening disrupted more than just the present."

Seth felt the gravity of her words anchor in his chest. Ro's lips pressed together. A new threat had entered the story—one beyond their understanding.

"The Time Stone," Seth repeated. "What does that mean for us?"

Lirien's reply was quiet, certain. "It means this isn't just a quest for the treasures. The Time Stone can move people across ages. Rewrite the flow of events. Whoever controls it could twist history."

Her gaze returned to the mountains beyond the window. "You're not just looking for the treasures, Seth. You're trying to prevent someone from using them to destroy everything."

A chill traced down Seth's spine. The journey had changed. The stakes had changed.

Ro stepped forward. "And you think someone from the future has it?"

"I don't know," Lirien admitted. "But the disturbances suggest someone has already begun to use it."

Seth looked at the shield in his hands. Its soft glow felt heavier now.

"We'll find the others," he said at last. "And stop whoever's behind this."

Lirien nodded. "Be careful. Your enemies won't always wear faces. Some forces can't be seen. And you'll need more than treasures to win."

Ro gave a half-smile. "Well… we've faced one creepy forest monster. That counts for something, right?"

Seth smiled faintly. Ember chirped from his shoulder, her amber eyes gleaming.

Lirien stepped closer, placing a hand on his shoulder. "I must leave as well. I need to reach the others—to stop them from doing something drastic, rather than risk them falling into the wrong hands. I have to remind them of their duty. Time is short."

Seth nodded. "I'll protect the treasures."

Lirien's expression softened. "It won't be easy to do alone. Find allies to help you. Just keep moving forward."

She turned toward the door. Seth and Ro followed, stepping into the morning light.

The road ahead was open. But no longer simple.

And somewhere in the future, someone was already watching.

The quest had truly begun.

Chapter 6

The Journey Begins

he road from Golden Arrow stretched out before them, winding through hills and dense forests, the sun casting long shadows as the day wore on. Seth and Ro walked side by side, their pace steady but their minds occupied with the uncertainty of the journey ahead.

Ro glanced at the amulet nestled in her pack. It had already guided her to Seth, to the shield—the first of the Nine Treasures. She had always kept it hidden, its power a secret. But now, it seemed the only way to find the rest of the treasures was to trust its magic.

"I think we should start using the amulet," Ro suggested, her voice low, unsure if Seth was ready to fully understand its significance. "It's how I found you, and how I found the shield. Maybe it will lead us to the next treasure."

Seth nodded, his thoughts aligning with hers. The amulet had already proven useful. "You're right. But we can't just rely on that alone. We need information—maps, legends, old stories. The bigger cities are probably our best bet for finding anything useful."

Ro raised an eyebrow, glancing over at him. "What cities do you have in mind?"

Seth thought for a moment. "Melbonia would be a good start. Lots of merchants come through there, and they hear all kinds of rumors. Zarnoth is another place with knowledge of history and magic. The City of Holodia has records—maybe even something about the treasures. Elsdone is hidden, but its magic users might have some clues. We could even head to Fergus if we have to, though it's dangerous. If anyone has information, it's there."

Ro's expression faltered slightly, a shadow passing over her face. Seth noticed her hesitation but didn't comment right away.

"What's wrong?" he asked, his voice soft, sensing her unease.

Ro bit her lip, then exhaled through her nose. "I just think it's risky. Bigger cities mean more eyes watching. Taverns, libraries, markets—places like that attract attention. And I don't exactly want to draw attention."

Seth frowned. "Why's that? We'll be discreet."

She let out a dry, humorless chuckle. "Because I'm wanted in most of them."

Seth blinked, startled. "Wait—what?"

Ro gave him a sideways glance, her tone sharp with a hint of sarcasm. "What, you think you're the first person I've ever stolen from?"

Seth opened his mouth to respond, then shut it. He wasn't sure if he was more surprised by her honesty or the way she said it —unapologetic, almost challenging.

"Look," she added, her voice softening slightly, "I'm not proud of all of it. But I've had to survive. And going into cities... that's just asking for trouble. Someone sees my face, remembers a poster or a job gone wrong—it could ruin everything."

She glanced at him again, smirking. "Just don't get any ideas about turning me in for a reward or anything."

Her tone was mocking, sarcastic—but there was a flicker of something else underneath it. A test. A warning. Maybe even a plea.

Seth was quiet for a moment, trying to make sense of what he'd just learned. She wasn't just a mysterious girl with a magical amulet—she had a past. A dangerous one.

"Alright," he said finally, his voice calm, "we'll be careful. We'll go to the bigger cities, but we'll lay low. You're right, we don't want to attract attention. Just stay close, and we'll stick together."

Ro gave him a tight smile, one that didn't quite reach her eyes. "Thanks, Seth. I'll be careful."

They continued their journey, both of them lost in thought, the weight of their unspoken words hanging between them. Seth had no idea just how much Ro was holding back, but he couldn't shake the feeling that she was hiding something important. He would find out, eventually. But for now, they had a quest to focus on.

They had no idea what dangers awaited them, but with the amulet guiding them and the possibility of hidden treasures in their future, they knew they had to keep moving forward.

Chapter 7

The Stranger in the Night

he night was quiet, save for the crackling of the

campfire and the occasional rustle of leaves in the wind. Seth sat cross-legged by the fire, sharpening his sword, the rhythmic scrape of metal on stone the only sound that filled the otherwise still air. Ember lay curled at his feet, her golden eyes glinting as she watched the surrounding forest, alert as always. Ro sat nearby, her back resting against a tree, her eyes scanning the woods, the ever-present tension of someone constantly on guard.

The firelight flickered, casting long shadows, when an eerie chill swept through the camp. It was sharp and unnatural, enough to make the hairs on the back of Seth's neck stand on end. Ember's head jerked up, her body tensing, while Ro instinctively reached for her dagger.

Seth slowly reached for his sword, his instincts telling him something was wrong. "Did you feel that?" he asked quietly, his voice low.

Ro nodded, her eyes narrowing as she scanned the darkened forest. "Yeah. Something's not right."

Then, the air before them shimmered, distorting like heat waves rising from the ground. Seth's grip on his sword tightened, and Ember growled softly, her wings twitching as if preparing for something.

A figure began to materialize in the midst of the shimmering air. It was faint at first, like a shadow stretching from the corners of a dream, its form fluid and ever-changing. Slowly, it solidified into something resembling a man, though its features were unclear, obscured by a dark, flowing cloak that billowed around it like smoke. A faint glow emanated from the figure, casting an unnatural light that made the fire seem dim in comparison.

Seth tensed, his eyes narrowing. "Who are you?" he demanded, his voice hard.

The figure didn't answer right away, instead standing still as though studying them both. Its presence felt heavy, like something ancient and powerful. Finally, it spoke, its voice deep and resonant, echoing in a way that made it seem like it was coming from more than one place at once.

"I am not here to harm you," the figure said, its voice carrying a strange undertone. "I have come to offer guidance."

Ro's hand remained on her dagger, her posture defensive. "Guidance?" she asked, her voice skeptical. "Who are you really?"

The figure took a step forward, its form flickering in and out of focus. "I am someone who knows the path you must follow. Someone who can help you find what you seek."

Seth glanced at Ro, then back at the figure. "What do you know about us?" he asked, his hand still resting on the hilt of his sword.

"I know you seek the treasures of the Nine Dragons," the figure replied. "And I know the one who can help you. You will need him. Zavalla."

"Zavalla?" he repeated. "What do you want with him?"

The figure paused, its gaze sweeping over them both. "Zavalla is... a key. He is the one who knows where the treasures are. But he is lost. He cannot reach them alone."

Seth frowned, confusion settling in. "What do you mean, 'lost'?"

The figure shifted slightly, its shape rippling like water disturbed by a breeze. "He is a sorcerer, one of great power, but he is crippled. He can no longer move as he once did. He needs help, and you will find him. He can guide you."

Ro's grip tightened on her dagger, her suspicion growing. "And why would we help him?" she asked, her voice sharp. "What makes him worth our time?"

The figure's eyes—if they could be called eyes—seemed to focus on Ro for a moment before it spoke again. "Because you will not find the treasures without him. Zavalla holds the knowledge you need. His fate is tied to your own, and without him, the path ahead will be unclear."

Seth studied the figure carefully, his mind racing. "Where do we find him?" he asked, determination creeping into his voice.

The figure seemed to consider this question carefully before replying. "Zavalla can be found near the ruins of Loopkin."

Ro shifted uneasily, still not fully trusting this apparition. "How do we know we can trust him? Or you?" she asked, her voice laced with doubt.

The figure seemed to smile, though its features remained indistinct. "Trust is a fragile thing. But know this—Zavalla holds the key to the knowledge you seek. Without him, you will be lost in the dark. And time is running out."

Seth's heart raced as the figure's words echoed in his mind. "We'll find him," he said, more to himself than anyone else.

The figure's form began to shimmer again, fading like mist in the wind. "Find him soon," it said, its voice distant now. "Before it is too late."

With that, the figure vanished, leaving only the faintest trace of its presence behind, like a whisper on the wind. The air seemed to return to normal, though the chill lingered for a moment longer.

Seth stood frozen for a moment, processing what had just happened. "What do you think?" he asked, turning to Ro.

She was silent for a moment, her expression unreadable. Finally, she spoke. "I don't know. But if what that thing said is true, we don't have much time. We have to find Zavalla."

Seth nodded, feeling the weight of the journey ahead pressing down on him. "Let's rest for the night. Tomorrow, we head to the ruins of Loopkin."

Ro glanced at the darkening forest, her gaze distant. "Tomorrow, then. But we stay sharp. Whatever that was, it wasn't human."

Seth turned back to the fire, trying to shake off the unease that settled over him. Ember stirred, sensing the tension, but curled back up against his legs, her warmth a small comfort in the growing darkness.

The night stretched on, quiet except for the sounds of the forest, and Seth couldn't help but feel that they were on the edge of something much larger than they could imagine. Their journey was just beginning, and there were far more dangers ahead than either of them had anticipated.

Chapter 8

Shadows of Loopkin

he sun crept over the ridges of the Impassable

Mountains as Seth, Ro, and Ember trudged along the winding trail, leaving behind the shelter of last night's camp. The strange midnight encounter with the shimmering figure—who claimed a crippled sorcerer named Zavalla needed help—still hung heavily in the air.

"He said he might know something about the treasures," Seth murmured for the third time that morning, running his fingers over the pink gemstone set in the center of his shield. "That can't be coincidence."

Ro said nothing. She kept her eyes forward, pretending to focus on the trail, but she was lost in thought. Something about the visitor's presence felt… wrong. Not dangerous, exactly, but out of place. Like he didn't belong in this time.

Ember, flapping lazily above them, gave a soft growl.

"I don't trust people who hide their faces in firelight," Ro, said. "It usually means they're hiding more than just their faces."

Seth nodded, though he didn't agree entirely. "He didn't seem like he wanted to hurt us. If what he said is true, this Zavalla might be the only one who can point us toward the next treasure."

Ro finally spoke. "Then let's go see him. But we stay sharp. Wizards can be clever, and not all of them have good intentions."

They turned southeast, following the long sloping roads that cut through the grasslands and into more craggy terrain. According to the stranger, Zavalla could be found near the ruins of Loopkin—a name that still stirred unease in the hearts of many.

Loopkin, once the pride of the realm, had been reduced to shattered towers and scorched stone long ago by the wrath of a great dragon. It was said the souls of the city's last defenders still lingered among the cracked arches and crumbling walls.

As they descended toward the ruined city, a dark silhouette loomed in the distance beyond the northern horizon—the jagged, unmistakable shape of Dragon Mountain. The stone dragon that crowned its peak stood frozen in a pose of fury, wings outstretched against the sky. Its shadow stretched long across the valley, casting a reminder of the force that had once destroyed Loopkin. The air around the mountain shimmered faintly, as if the power that turned the beast to stone still lingered.

Ro stared up at the mountain with a strange intensity.

"I've heard stories about the Red Dragon," she said quietly. "My father told them to me when I was little—before things got complicated." She glanced at Seth. "They say the dragon that destroyed Loopkin wasn't wild. It was summoned—or perhaps angered. Some claim it had ties to the throne of Zarnoth. Others say it came looking for something that was stolen."

She hesitated, sorting through half-remembered tales. "The City of Zarnoth was built after Loopkin fell. Since then,

57

Zarnoth has been at odds with the Fergoes. That rivalry... it goes back to when Loopkin fell."

Seth listened as she continued, her tone shifting between curiosity and uncertainty.

"Loopkin was a place of wonders—wealth, peace, magic. But the stories say greed crept in. The king feared magic, feared other races. He mistreated his people, drove many out. One of the Grand Knights, Uransus Loktose, tried to start a new kingdom. He wanted peace, even married the princess to seal it. But something went wrong. A dragon came. Burned it all."

"Do they say why?" Seth asked.

Ro shook her head slowly. "No. That part is always… vague. No one knows for sure why it attacked. Some say the dragon was summoned by a betrayed soul. Others whisper the dragon was seeking justice."

"Do you believe it?"

"I believe something powerful was angry. And I believe Bobooshkin the Wizard turned the dragon to stone to save what was left. That dragon—now Dragon Mountain—isn't just a mountain. It's a scar."

"Do you think the Red Dragon's treasure is up there?" Seth asked.

"I think the Red Dragon *is* the treasure," Ro replied. "Turned to stone and still guarding something none of us understand."

By dusk, the ruins came into view.

Blackened stone spires rose like jagged teeth from the earth. Vines wrapped around broken columns, and the remains of once-grand archways cast long shadows in the dying light. Wind howled softly through the ruins, carrying with it whispers that didn't belong to the breeze.

They made camp on the outskirts, just outside what had once been Loopkin's grand marketplace. As Seth arranged their small fire and Ember curled up to nap, Ro stepped away to scout the area.

That was when she saw him.

A figure, seated beneath the remains of a fallen statue—hunched, cloaked, still.

She approached carefully, hand near her dagger. "Are you Zavalla?"

The man didn't move for a moment, then slowly turned his head. One eye, glowing faintly, met hers. The other—scarred, blind—remained still.

"You found me," the man rasped.

Ro relaxed only slightly. "We were told you might know something about the Nine Treasures."

A bitter chuckle. "Told by whom?"

She hesitated. "He didn't give a name. But he looked… like a ghost. A shimmer. Maybe a spirit."

Zavalla's eyes narrowed, though he said nothing for a while. Then: "That explains the dreams."

She arched a brow. "Dreams?"

"I've seen things—places I've never been, voices I've never heard. Whispers of power, colors that don't exist in this world. I thought it was madness." He paused. "Perhaps I was wrong."

She motioned for Seth and Ember, and soon the group sat together, listening as the crippled sorcerer told them what he knew.

"The treasures exist," Zavalla confirmed. "And I may have… fragments. Of where they are. Not from maps or scrolls, but from visions. And riddles left in the ruins of the old world."

Seth leaned forward. "Then we need your help. If you can remember anything, even small clues, they could guide us."

Zavalla tapped the side of his head. "It's all in here. Jumbled. But I can feel the pull of them. One of them—one shaped like a crown—sings to me from the ocean."

Seth's eyes widened. "The Aquarian Crown."

Ro reached into her cloak and pulled out the Amnathoth Amulet. Its ruby center flickered faintly, the coiled gold dragon around it seeming almost to shift in the firelight.

Zavalla's eyes locked on it. "You carry the Amnathoth."

She tucked it away. "It led me to Seth. Maybe it can lead us to the others."

Zavalla nodded slowly. "Then go. Head to the Port of Melbonia. There, you'll find someone who can take you across the sea."

Seth exchanged glances with Ro. "Someone trustworthy?"

A long pause.

"Prehaps," Zavalla said. "Someone who's willing."

Zavalla stood slowly, leaning on a twisted staff. "And I'll come with you," he added. "I may be broken, but I can still be useful. And if my dreams mean anything… this journey isn't just yours anymore. It's mine, too."

The group was silent for a beat, then Ro nodded. "Then let's not waste time."

Together, they turned their eyes toward the road ahead—toward Melbonia, the sea, and whatever waited beyond the crashing waves.

Zavalla now walked among them, silent but thoughtful, a figure cloaked in mystery and shadow. His presence marked a turning point, though none yet understood how deep his role in this tale would run.

Chapter 9

The Road to Melbonia

he morning sun stretched over the hills of Acklelend,

casting long shadows as Seth, Ro, Ember, and their newest companion, Zavalla, left behind the haunted ruins of Loopkin. The Impassible Mountains were now far to the north, their snow-capped peaks just faint silhouettes on the horizon.

They traveled southward across the great meadows, following old trade roads that had fallen into disrepair. The terrain was dry and golden, with the wind rustling tall grass and distant herds of horned lempra grazing peacefully. Occasionally, a rockworm would churn up from beneath the gravel path, startled by their footsteps, only to retreat again into the earth.

Zavalla walked slower than the rest, leaning on his twisted staff, but he never complained. He observed everything—cloud patterns, the movement of birds, the shapes of trees. Seth had begun to notice how sharp the old man's mind was, even if his body had been broken.

By midday, they reached a shaded grove near a small spring. There, they rested. Ro knelt by the water, checking the amulet she wore. The ruby in its center glowed faintly—more often now than before.

"Still pointing south," she muttered.

"We're going the right way," Seth said, rinsing his face in the water. "Melbonia should only be a few days off. If the Amnathoth Amulet keeps leading us, we'll get there."

Zavalla looked thoughtful. "The sea holds many secrets. It will test you."

"What do you mean?" Seth asked.

But Zavalla only shook his head. "You'll understand soon enough."

That night, they made camp beneath the stars in the foothills near the forest of Gullen Pines. Ember kept watch, occasionally letting out a quiet growl to warn off nearby creatures. The wind whispered through the grasslands as the group settled into uneasy sleep, the road ahead heavy with unseen promise.

The journey to Melbonia had begun—and with it, the first steps toward the Aquarian Crown hidden across the sea.

They continued southward through the rolling fields and quiet hills of Acklelend.

Before reaching the Port of Melbonia—one of the two major cities of the region, alongside Holodia—the group would have to pass near the fringes of the territory of Mar.

Both Melbonia and Mar were governed by powerful regional lords under the broader rule of the Zarnothian Crown. While Melbonia remained largely loyal to Zarnoth, the leadership in Mar had long harbored quiet resentment, their banners often flown with more pride than allegiance. Tensions simmered between these outlands and the throne, and though the group would avoid the heart of Mar if they could, trade routes still wove close to its borders.

It was a cool morning as they made their way along a wooded path, quiet but for the crunch of dry leaves underfoot. Seth walked ahead, Ember striding freely beside him, untethered and alert. Ro walked beside him, holding the amulet that glowed faintly with its ruby light.

"Seth," Ro said softly, breaking the silence. "Back in Golden Arrow… your mother said something about your father. That he was a great adventurer."

Seth hesitated, looking at the horizon. "Yeah. Romos Bergan. He was one of the best—or so everyone says. He died protecting Golden Arrow from a raid by the Modo hill tribes when I was nine."

"I'm sorry," Ro said gently. "I never knew my mother. And my father… let's just say he sees people more as pieces on a game board than family."

Seth glanced at her but didn't pry. He could tell there was more to her story, but she wasn't ready to share it yet.

Behind them, Zavalla slowed his pace, watching Seth carefully. He had been quiet since they left Loopkin, processing what he had learned.

"So," he finally said, "your mother… she's one of the Nine Dragons of Existence."

Seth turned, startled. "How do you—?"

"I can sense it now. Her presence is etched into you," Zavalla said. "That means you're Dragonkin, like me."

"Dragonkin?" Seth asked, frowning. "What does that even mean?"

"It means power—untamed, ancient power. It means your blood carries the memory of creation itself," Zavalla said. "My father was one of the dragons, too. The Red Dragon."

Seth blinked. "So… we're both…"

"Half-human. Half-legend," Zavalla said with a faint smile. "Though our paths have been very different."

Ro stared at him, stunned. "The Red Dragon? The one that destroyed Loopkin?"

Zavalla nodded. "Yes. He was betrayed, twisted by grief and vengeance. He burned the city, and Bobooshkin turned him to stone to stop him."

Seth felt the weight of his shield against his back. "Then… Dragon Mountain. That's your father?"

Zavalla turned his eyes toward the horizon. "What's left of him."

A heavy silence settled over them. Ro was the first to speak again.

"Why didn't you say anything sooner?"

Zavalla's voice was calm, but his eyes were distant. "Because truths like that… they carry weight. And not everyone is ready to bear them. I kept it hidden because I had to—because it made me a target. And because I didn't want to believe it."

Ro narrowed her eyes. "But how are you still alive? That battle happened generations ago."

Zavalla smiled faintly, though it didn't quite reach his eyes. "I've had... help. Spells that slow aging. Potions lost to time.

Deals I'd rather not speak of. Some say time flows in one direction—I've found that to be… negotiable."

He turned away before either of them could press further. Seth wasn't sure if Zavalla was telling the truth—or just the part he wanted them to know.

Seth looked down at the pink gem in his shield, feeling its warmth pulse faintly. "My mother is the Pink Dragon."

Zavalla's head tilted slightly, and his eye narrowed. "Then we're not so different, you and I."

Ro looked between them. "You're both Dragonkin. No wonder you're drawn to the treasures. No wonder you felt the call."

"I didn't ask for this," Seth said.

"Neither did I," Zavalla replied. "But maybe that's why we were chosen."

They walked in silence for a while, the sea breeze cutting between them. Each of them now carried a greater understanding—and a greater burden.

Ro's voice cut through the silence. "Whatever you two are, dragon-blooded or not, we need to find this smuggler. The world won't save itself."

Zavalla glanced at Seth. "If you want, I can teach you. Magic, I mean. But be warned—our kind… using magic isn't always safe. Channeling too much too soon, or without control, can awaken parts of you that aren't human. It can change you. Make you more dragon than man."

Seth looked down at his hands, quiet. The idea both frightened and intrigued him.

Ro glanced ahead at the distant city walls of Mar. Her posture stiffened, and her voice dropped low. "We need to move quickly through these parts. I… just have a bad feeling."

Seth noticed the tension in her expression, the way her eyes scanned every distant shape. She was nervous—afraid of being recognized, though she wouldn't say why.

The shadow of Mar loomed ahead.

They traveled on beneath overcast skies, the clouds casting moving shadows over the uneven hills of southern Acklelend. The scent of damp earth and wild herbs drifted through the air, and Ember moved with watchful confidence, her claws barely making a sound on the packed dirt path.

As they made camp near a cluster of mossy boulders just before twilight, the fire crackled quietly, its warmth welcome in the rising chill. Seth sat near the flames, holding the shield on his lap, its pink gem catching and reflecting the flickering light. Across from him, Zavalla sat in silence until finally he spoke.

"There's something you need to understand about what you are," Zavalla said. "Being Dragonkin… it changes things. If you use magic—especially without control—it can alter your form."

"Alter how?" Seth asked.

Zavalla raised his right hand and slowly pulled back his sleeve. His forearm shimmered faintly in the firelight—part of his skin bore the sheen of scaled red flesh, glinting like embers.

"This," he said, "is what happens when you tap into the deeper currents of magic as a Dragonkin. You become closer to what's inside you… more dragon than man, if you're not careful."

Seth stared. "Does it hurt?"

"Not in the way you'd think. But it's a reminder. Magic isn't just power—it's identity. And it comes at a price."

Seth was quiet for a moment, then asked, "Is that why… your legs…?"

Zavalla looked into the fire. "No. That was something else. A long time ago, in a city, a group called the PAW—the People Against Wizards—caught me in an alley. They hate all magic, and they hate anything tied to the dragons even more. They beat me near to death. Broke my legs. Burned part of my face. I was just a boy then. I've never walked the same since."

Ro looked up from across the fire, a flicker of anger in her eyes. "That's horrible."

Zavalla gave a grim smile. "There are many in this world who still carry the fear and hate left behind from when the dragons tried to wipe out humanity. People don't forget being nearly destroyed. And they don't forgive."

Seth looked down at the shield in his hands, the dragon-forged emblem of protection and empathy. He thought about his mother—her scales, her power, her sadness. And what it meant to be part of something so old, and so feared.

With the shield in his lap, Seth felt something stir deep inside —a strange echo that resonated with Zavalla's pain. A thread of emotion, not his own. Empathy. He could feel the weight Zavalla carried. The shame. The yearning. The quiet suffering masked by sarcasm and grim resolve.

"But you learned magic anyway," Seth said.

Zavalla nodded. "I did. And I can teach you. But you must choose how much of yourself you're willing to risk. I'm looking for the green treasure—Gauntlets of Verdance. They say it can heal and restore life. Maybe it can fix what PAW left broken in me."

The fire popped, sending a brief spray of sparks into the night. No one spoke for a while after that. The road ahead felt longer now, heavier with truth.

And the city of Melbonia still waited in the distance.

Chapter 10

Approaching Mar

The hills gradually gave way to marshy lowlands as the group descended into the mist-laden realm of Mar. This land, infamous among traders and travelers, was wide and wet —an expanse of mossy ridges, moors, and deep peat bogs. It lay tucked in a basin surrounded by storied regions: to the east, the gnarled limbs of the Dark Swamp stretched toward the horizon like grasping claws; beyond that, the strange bioluminescent canopy of the Dark Forest shimmered faintly under a grey sky. To the northeast, the edges of the Impassable Mountains vanished into cold mist. And to the southwest lay the more inviting territory of Melbonia, with its merchant roads and fertile hills, where the famed City of Holodia and the bustling Port of Melbonia awaited.

An old, half-sunken trade path led them southward, threading around shallow ponds and broken stone bridges long lost to time. Water pooled underfoot and reeds brushed against their legs. Birds with haunting cries circled overhead while frogs croaked ominous warnings from beneath thick ferns.

Ember, Seth's small Lomek dragon, darted between low-flying branches and hummocks of earth, wings fluttering in rhythmic bursts. Occasionally, she landed atop Seth's shoulder, chirping in satisfaction or trilling short, melodic notes—her way of keeping watch. Once, she snapped at a buzzing insect with a sharp twist of his head, then chirped proudly.

"I still can't believe she's so small," Ro remarked with a smirk. "She looks like he should be nestled in a tea kettle."

"She's more capable than she looks," Seth replied, scratching the soft scales under Ember's chin. "She senses things we can't. She's already picked up on when we're being watched."

They stopped near a crooked stone marker almost lost beneath layers of moss and ivy. The runes were faint, but enough to mark the outer boundaries of Mar. The actual city, a sprawl deeper in the mists, was avoided by most who valued their safety or secrets.

"We're not going in," Ro said, gaze locked on the fog-draped horizon. "We'll skirt the edge of the territory. Trust me, that city holds more danger than comfort."

Seth looked at her curiously. "Guess you've been here before, stole from here also?"

Ro hesitated, then shrugged. "Let's just say my feet walked off with something they wanted… badly. Mar doesn't forget its secrets—or its faces."

Zavalla, riding beside them atop a conjured mountain ram with thick fur and curling black horns, remained quiet. He scanned the moorland with a wary eye, then turned his attention to Seth.

"You've grown," he observed. "Even your connection to the shield... it's more visible now."

Seth shifted the weight of the rose-gem shield strapped across his back. "It's hard to describe. It's like it knows things before I do. Like it feels what I feel. Or maybe I feel what it feels."

"That's the magic of it," Zavalla said softly. "Your blood, your purpose, your destiny—they're tied to it. It doesn't just protect. It understands."

He let the words hang, lost in thought. A long silence followed as the group continued through patches of dry stone and sinking mud.

"The world isn't kind to magic," Zavalla continued at last. "And it's far crueler to those with dragonblood. There are old hatreds... ones that never died out."

Seth looked over. "Like the PAW?"

""They believe magic is a curse, that dragons are monsters. They call people like us abominations." Zavalla replied grimly. "Their hatred is deep. Ancient. In some places, they act in the open. Here... they skulk in the shadows."

Ro glanced back. "They're active in this part of the land?"

"They are cowards and move in groups," Zavalla said. "They prey on fear. They twist old truths and turn them into fuel for violence."

He adjusted the way he sat in the saddle, and a slight grimace crossed his face.

"They found me once," he said after a pause. "Left me broken. Not just in body, but in spirit. And that's why I seek the green treasure," he continued. "Nature's breath. Life magic. It may be the only thing left that can restore what they took."

The shield pulsed gently on Seth's back, a flush of sorrow rising in his chest—not his own, but something shared. Zavalla's pain radiated through the artifact like an echo.

72

Seth didn't speak. He simply listened.

The mist thickened as the path twisted around a small pond
with reeds that whispered in the breeze. Strange lights flickered
in the distance—fireflies or something stranger, their glow
flickering like silent warnings in the fog.

Ro pulled her hood low. "We're getting close to the Melbonian
border. We should move quicker."

Seth nodded. "No point in camping here."

And so they moved forward—quiet and deliberate—through
the haunted moors of Mar. They would not enter the city, but
the shadow of its presence loomed all the same. With each step,
the land seemed to watch them, waiting to see who they would
become.

Chapter 11

Through the Borderlands

The sun was beginning to pierce the morning mists as
the group made their way out of the far edge of the Mar
wetlands. With each step, the ground became more solid, and
the air gradually shifted from the clammy breath of the bogs to
the drier, brisk wind sweeping inland from the plains of
Melbonia. Though the marshes of Mar remained behind them,
a sense of unease still clung to the group like the stubborn fog
that trailed their boots. The region of Mar, with its moors and
dark peat bogs, had a way of sinking into one's bones—a land
too full of memory and sorrow to be left behind easily.

"How far to Holodia from here?" Seth asked as he adjusted his
pack.

Ro consulted a weatherworn map she had stashed in her cloak.
"Two, maybe three days if the roads are still intact. That's
assuming we don't hit trouble. Bandits like to roam this
stretch."

Zavalla, ever quiet, simply nodded. His conjured ram walked
beside them with an unsettling stillness, its hooves making no
sound on the hardened ground.

Ember soared overhead in lazy spirals, occasionally dipping
down to ride on Seth's shoulder. The little Lomek dragon

clicked his jaws, eyes scanning the skies. Despite his small size, he carried himself like a guardian.

The group passed into an area known to travelers as the Borderlands—a wide swath of flat, rolling plains and scattered thickets, dotted with the remains of ancient stone outposts left behind from wars long past. Half-crumbled watchtowers and vine-strangled waystones whispered of a time when Zarnoth and the Fergo had fought bitterly over this stretch of land.

They took rest beneath one such broken tower. The wind had picked up, whistling through the broken stone and flapping the corners of Ro's cloak as she sat cross-legged beside the fire. Sparks occasionally flared upward like fireflies caught in the breeze.

Seth poked at the flames. "You never really told me what your father was like."

Ro looked up, startled. Her gaze drifted for a moment, thoughtful.

"He was... involved in things I never understood," she said carefully. "Important to a lot of people. Respected, feared. He always seemed more focused on duty than on being a father. Always watching, always calculating. I used to think he was cold, but now... I think he was just scared. Of what might happen if he lost control."

"You don't sound angry."

"I'm not. Not anymore. But I left because I wanted to be something more than a pawn in someone else's plans."

Seth looked at her for a long moment, then gave a quiet nod.

From where he sat tuning the crystal embedded in his staff, Zavalla suddenly spoke. "You made your choice, Ro. That's a power most never grasp. But it will also make you dangerous to those who think they know your place."

Ro gave a dry chuckle. "Isn't that always the way?"

They camped that night beside a wind-bent willow tree, its roots curled like sleeping animals around ancient stone slabs. Ember curled on Seth's chest, his warm breath a comfort in the cool night. Overhead, stars glittered through the shifting cloud cover. Distant howls echoed from the east—perhaps wolves, perhaps something older.

Zavalla didn't sleep. He sat apart from the others, his eyes locked on the stars. The fire cast his shadow in long, dragon-like shapes against the stones. Whatever thoughts haunted him, he did not share them. But Seth noticed the way the older man's gaze lingered north, toward the places none of them dared name aloud.

At dawn, they broke camp and resumed their journey. The roads ahead grew more defined, carved deeper by wagon wheels and trade caravans. Birds called from the high trees. The scents of mint and dry grass rode the wind. Occasionally, they passed shepherd stones etched with glyphs from the Nowin tongue—wardings against spirits, reminders that even here, magic had touched the land long ago.

As they entered deeper into Melbonia, signs of its unique ecology began to appear. The group passed a field of Tokoon palms—tall stalks with dense, leafy fronds that shaded clusters of dark purple fruit shaped like tight, bush-like fists. The fruit was salty, nutritious, and a staple food across Acklelend— except to Lopkins, for whom it was deadly poison.

Near the palms, a group of Melborats scurried through the underbrush. About two feet long with six legs and furless, mottled skin, the creatures shifted colors as they moved—one turning light blue as the others stayed gray.

"Looks like fair weather tomorrow," Ro noted.

Seth raised an eyebrow. "Because of their color?"

"Melborats," Ro explained. "They predict the weather. Tokoon farmers use them all the time. That one turning blue means clear skies. Pretty reliable for something that looks like a cross between a rat and a potato."

The road sloped downward toward a broad valley, and as they topped a low ridge, they saw it at last: the first glinting towers of Holodia faint on the horizon, framed by distant waterfalls and rising mist.

Holodia was unlike any other city in Acklelend. Built in tiers into the cliffs and canyons carved by the mighty Twinfall Rivers, its towers and stone bridges gleamed silver in the morning light. The city thrummed with steam and machinery— water-powered forges, rotating windmills, and massive gears spun by harnessed waterfalls. Blacksmiths, tinkerers, and inventors filled its bustling levels, the scent of hot iron mingling with fresh mountain air. Plumes of white vapor rose from chimneys like breath from a sleeping titan.

From here, the city's outline resembled a great anvil crowned by steam. Trade caravans snaked toward its gates, and high above, the occasional gleam of a glider could be seen coasting from one tower to the next, carried by the mountain wind. Bells chimed at regular intervals, marking the shift hours at the forges and mills.

It was a place of craft and innovation, but also of secrets and shadows. And for the group, it was the next step on their journey—a crossroads where invention met ambition, and stories often shifted course.

They had reached the true edge of Melbonia.

Chapter 12

Smoke and Steel

he air in Holodia crackled with life. Steam hissed

from every corner, rising from vents in the cobblestone streets and the massive stone forges built into the cliffs. The roar of hammers striking metal echoed across the city tiers like thunder trapped in a canyon. Gleaming pipework and narrow rails snaked between towering workshops and bustling markets. Here, invention wasn't a luxury—it was the law of survival.

Seth looked around in awe as they passed a merchant square where bronze automata with whirring gears polished swords, and smiths doused glowing iron into steaming troughs. Ember clung tight to his shoulder, wide-eyed and wary of the many contraptions.

Just before they entered the square, Seth noticed a cluster of old wanted posters peeling from a rusted noticeboard by a gear-driven message kiosk. Most were torn or stained by soot—but a few faces still lingered in the paper grain. One had long, dark hair and a shadowed hood. The resemblance to Ro made him glance her way.

Curious, he stepped toward the board for a better look.

Before he could get close, Ro rushed over, yanked the poster down, and tore it into pieces, casting quick glances over her shoulder to be sure no one was watching. The shredded paper fluttered into a nearby drain.

79

Seth raised his eyebrows. "Wow. You really are wanted."

Ro spun on him and pressed a finger to his lips. "Shh. Not here."

She tugged her hood even lower and turned sharply into a narrow alley. "Let's just say Holodia's not the kind of place I like being seen." Her voice was low and tight. "Too many eyes. Too many people who like to remember things for money."

Zavalla's gaze swept across the city like a hawk watching from above. "If we're going to find word of the next treasure, this is the place," he said. "Smiths trade stories for metal, and scholars drink with mercenaries. There's truth here, hidden in the noise."

They made their way to the lower tiers where the taverns and trade halls buzzed with conversation. At the base of the third tier, nestled under an arch of carved stone, stood a ramshackle building with copper-plated windows and a crooked sign that read *The Anvil & Ember*.

Inside, it was warm and dark, the air thick with the scent of oil, ale, and forge soot. Workers crowded the tables, swapping stories and tossing dice between greasy plates. At the bar, a bald woman with soot-stained gloves was loudly arguing with a man in a metal breastplate about who made the better blade— Holodians or the dwarves.

Ro scanned the room and nodded toward a quiet table in the back. "Let's sit. Keep your ears open."

As they took their seats, a tall figure at the bar drew Ro's attention.

He had a jagged scar across one cheek, a long coat stained by salt and blood, and a strange mechanism strapped to his belt.

The man spoke in hushed tones to the barkeep, who leaned in and pointed toward a shadowy corner of the tavern where a map was pinned on the wall.

They couldn't hear the full conversation, but Ro's ears sharpened when the name *Lost Island* was mentioned.

"I've heard of that place," the man muttered, "waterfalls all around it. No ordinary ship can reach it. But I've got a line on a captain with the nerve and the vessel."

The barkeep grunted. "Thalen Greaves?"

"That's the one."

Ro leaned closer to Seth. "Did you hear that? He's talking about the Lost Island. The place with the waterfalls. That has to be where the Aquarian Crown is."

Zavalla's eyes narrowed. "And that's Zarcan Lawnbar."

Seth gave him a blank look. "Who?"

Ro kept her voice low. "I've heard of him. He was raised by pirates, learned to fight before he could read. They say he killed half his crew before being tossed overboard and left for dead."

"Clearly he didn't die," Zavalla said.

"No," Ro said. "Now he takes mercenary work. Anything for gold. They say he's ruthless—but he always finds what he's looking for."

They stayed quiet, pretending to drink while keeping an eye on Zarcan. He moved toward the map on the wall, studying the sea routes drawn there. Then he tapped it, grinning.

"If Thalen Greaves is in Port Melbonia," Zarcan said to no one in particular, "I'm getting that ship. And nothing's stopping me."

He turned and strode out, boots echoing on the floor.

Ro exhaled. "Now we know where to go. And we know who's after the treasure too."

"Let's hope we get there before he does," Seth said.

Outside, Holodia churned on—smoke rising, steel ringing. Beneath it all, secrets stirred in the steam.

And the treasure hunt had truly begun.

Just south of Holodia, nestled between towering stone cliffs and the shimmering coastal waters, lay Port Melbonia. The journey from the city's steam-choked forges to the salt-sweet breeze of the docks took little more than an hour, the roads winding past seaside mills and weather-beaten wind towers. Sailcloth flapped in the wind, gulls screamed overhead, and the scent of the sea filled their lungs.

Chapter 13

The Rusty Turtle

The road from Holodia to Port Melbonia wound down
from the steaming cliffs to the low coastal wetlands, where
gulls wheeled overhead and the scent of salt began to replace
the tang of metal and smoke. The city of steel and steam faded
behind them, its towers receding into the haze as rolling hills
gave way to flatter, wind-brushed terrain.

They passed through dense patches of red-leafed bristlebark
trees and fields lined with coils of shimmering grass, silver-
tipped and swaying with each breeze. The land grew softer, the
earth damp beneath their boots. Narrow wooden bridges
carried them across winding streams, and every so often, the
distant bellow of a foghorn reminded them they were nearing
the sea.

The trip didn't take more than half a day, but the change in
atmosphere was stark. Holodia's roar of hammers and machines
faded, replaced by the rhythmic cries of gulls and the creaking
moans of docked ships rocked gently by the tide.

Finally, the road opened up to reveal Port Melbonia—a coastal
sprawl of warehouses, crooked harbormaster towers, salt-
streaked taverns, and a sea of sails fluttering in the salty breeze.
The port smelled of brine and burnt oil. Sailors shouted from
every direction, unloading wares or hawking jobs. Stacks of
crates, barrels, and coils of rope lined the harbor road, bustling
with life. The heart of the port pulsed with life—fishermen
haggled, traders unloaded crates of glimmering goods, and

shipwrights hammered repairs into vessels moored along the wharves.

But it was the tavern at the far end of the docks that caught their eye.

Nestled at the edge of the harbor, partially sunken into the sand and stone, loomed a strange and ancient sight: The Rusty Turtle.

It stood half-buried in the earth, the hull of an ancient mechanical sea turtle—once a massive submarine forged by a forgotten civilization. Its bronze plating was weathered green and coppery, barnacles clinging to what was once a reinforced shell. The head of the turtle—wide-eyed and hollow—rested just above the entrance, its jaw lowered like a drawbridge to welcome patrons inside.

Iron pipes jutted from its shell like chimneys, puffing out steam with a faint hiss. Its once-movable flippers had been repurposed into awnings, shielding outdoor tables from rain and sun. Etched along the rusted metal were strange runes from a time before dragons laid waste to the world. A faded menu was carved into a salvaged hull plate near the entrance, listing drinks with names like "Kraken's Gullet" and "Boiled Gnome."

From inside, the eerie tones of a sea-song whistled through old speaker tubes—half haunting, half mechanical. Patrons came and went with nervous glances, speaking in hushed tones as if the turtle itself were listening.

"This place…" Ro whispered. "It's a relic."

Seth raised an eyebrow. "And a bar?"

Zavalla smirked. "Only in Melbonia."

They crossed the turtle's metal jaw and stepped inside.

The interior was no less bizarre—faded bronze walls lined with warped metal furniture, steam hissing from valves in the corners. The bar itself had been carved from an old engine casing, with bottles tucked into the ribs of the turtle's inner frame. Copper chandeliers hung from overhead struts, casting amber light through the warm haze. Behind the bar stood a heavyset woman with a monocle fused to her left eye socket, pouring drinks with uncanny speed while occasionally barking orders to a dwarven server with gears embedded in his apron.

Ro led them to a quiet table near the back, careful not to attract too much attention.

From the bar, a familiar voice rumbled, low and gritty.

"I heard he's docked today. Captain Thalen Greaves. Has a ship that can reach unreachable locations."

The speaker leaned close to the bartender, his black-gloved hand gripping a tankard. A long coat draped over his broad shoulders, and a jagged scar split his face. A strange weapon— half cutlass, half sawblade—hung at his side, its hilt etched with the markings of old pirate clans.

As he spoke, a hush fell over the nearby tables. Conversations paused. Eyes shifted away. Even the barkeep's voice dropped to a near whisper.

Seth leaned toward Ro and whispered, "That's the guy we saw in Holodia, isn't it?"

Ro nodded, her eyes never leaving him. "Zarcan Lawnbar. Mercenary, smuggler... dangerous man. I've heard things."

Zavalla frowned. "We're sure we want to follow him?"

Ro hesitated. "We don't have to follow him—just get ahead of him. He's after something, and I think it's the same thing we are."

"We need that ship," Zavalla said. "If anyone can get to the Lost Island, it's Greaves. And if Zarcan's going after him… we'd best be ahead of him."

Zarcan finished his drink, murmured something else to the barkeep, then turned and exited without a glance back. Patrons slowly resumed their conversations, but the tension lingered like stormclouds.

Ro stood, eyes narrowed. "Let's find Greaves before he does."

The hunt for the blue dragon's treasure was on   and the sea, wild and unforgiving, awaited.

Chapter 14

Wings on the Water

he next morning brought sea mist and the sound of

gulls screaming over the rooftops of Port Melbonia. The harbor bustled with activity—sailors unloading crates, merchants shouting offers, and ships bobbing against their moorings like restless beasts.

Ro, Seth, and Zavalla made their way through the crowd with purpose. It didn't take long to find the vessel they were looking for.

Moored at the farthest end of the dock sat a strange and magnificent ship, one that looked like it had been pulled from the bones of a forgotten age. The vessel was forged entirely from dull bronze and dark iron, its surface pitted and scarred by time. This was the Stormrider, a salvaged relic from the world before dragons tore civilization apart.

Its hull shimmered with patches of lomek-hide sewn between armored plating—repairs made long after its original creators had vanished. Steam vents puffed intermittently from along its spine, and thick cables of copper ran from bow to stern, pulsing faintly with a rhythmic, magical glow. The sails, instead of fabric, were woven sheets of glinting metal thread and rune-etched crystal, stretching out like wings ready to unfurl.

"Stormrider," Seth said aloud, eyes wide. "Looks more machine than ship."

"Some say it flew once," Ro murmured. "A remnant from the ancient war. One of the sky-ships that crossed oceans and storms like birds cross rivers."

A gruff voice caught their attention. A tall sailor with a belt full of navigation tools and a gaze sharp as a hooked blade was calling out from the deck.

"We're short three crew for the next leg! Strong backs, quick feet—apply with Second

 Mate Elgan at the quarterdeck!"

Seth exchanged a glance with Ro and Zavalla. "This might be our chance."

Ro nodded. "We get aboard as crew, stay low, and don't cause trouble. That way, no one's tossing us into the sea."

They approached the boarding ramp, where a wiry man with sea-stained gloves and a mechanical spyglass tucked behind one ear was scribbling names into a ledger.

"Names?" he barked.

"Roth," Seth said quickly. "These are my cousins."

Zavalla raised a brow but said nothing.

The man—Elgan—gave them a long look, then nodded. "Fine. You'll work your keep. Deck scrubbing, rope coiling, and hold watch. You cause trouble, you swim."

Seth was assigned to basic labor roles—deck scrubbing and rope duty. Zavalla, after some hesitation from Elgan, was assigned to assist the navigator.

"You don't look like you can coil a rope or lift a barrel."

Zavalla met his gaze evenly. "I've got eyes. I see patterns. I read stars."

Elgan frowned, considering. "Fine. Chart duties. You'll assist the navigator and interpret the arc-lens when it flares. You mess up, we hit rocks, you answer to the Captain."

As for Ro, she was handed a wooden spoon and directed below deck.

"Kitchen duty," Elgan said, jerking a thumb toward the galley. "Cook could use an extra pair of hands."

Ro opened her mouth to protest, then thought better of it. She disappeared down the narrow stairwell, her footsteps echoing.

They signed their names and were led aboard. The Stormrider's deck was a flurry of motion. Ropes swung, gears clicked, and sea-charmed anchors hissed steam as they were drawn up.

Ro ran her hand along the patched metal and weathered lomek-hide of the hull. "I can't believe we made it."

"Let's not get ahead of ourselves," Zavalla muttered. "Now we just have to make sure we stay on it."

What she didn't expect was to find the cook was a boy barely older than she was—freckled, tall, and heavy set, with sharp eyes that flicked toward her as she entered. He was already shouting at a pot that seemed to be boiling over of its own accord. He introduced himself as Milo, and though he clearly didn't appreciate the sudden help, there was a spark of curiosity—or mischief—lingering behind his frown.

Below deck, the ship creaked and groaned like some great ancient beast awakening. But above, the sails caught the wind and magic alike, and the Stormrider surged from the harbor like a forgotten god reborn.

They were on their way to the Lost Island.

Chapter 15

Secrets at Sea

he Stormrider was unlike any ship still sailing—or perhaps soaring—through the seas of Acklelend. Forged from bronze and dark iron, patched with glimmering lomek-hide, and powered by forgotten arcane machinery, it thrummed with a pulse older than memory. The metal sails shimmered like dragonfly wings, humming softly as they drank the wind and magic alike. Its decks were lined with aged brass fixtures and glass domes filled with swirling light, casting moving shadows as the ship cut through the waves.

Below deck, Ro found herself elbow-deep in the chaos of the galley.

"Watch the flame, don't stir counterclockwise, and whatever you do, don't touch that pot," Milo barked, pointing to a cauldron with steam rising in colored spirals.

Ro blinked. "Why not?"

"Because it bites," Milo said flatly, smirking. "New to this, aren't you?"

He was tall and broad-shouldered, barely older than she was, with freckles across his nose and sharp green eyes that missed nothing. His hair was a mop of red curls, damp with sweat from the heat of the stoves. As Ro chopped vegetables with unfamiliar grace, Milo glanced her way again, this time lingering a little too long.

"You've got nice posture for a galley hand," he said, voice casual. "Kind of royal, even."

Ro stiffened. "Excuse me?"

He just shrugged, lips quirking in a faint smile. "Nothing. Just saying. You carry yourself like someone who's had... proper training."

Ro met his gaze, her expression carefully neutral. Milo didn't press the matter further, but the sparkle in his eyes told her he'd guessed something. Not everything—but enough.

Above deck, the Stormrider surged forward under full power. Copper veins along its hull glowed steadily, and the crystal inlays on its wheel pulsed with direction. Seth and Zavalla worked alongside the crew—Seth running ropes and learning knots with blistered hands, Zavalla assisting the navigator in the chart room, interpreting readings from a flickering arc-lens that responded to celestial bodies.

It wasn't long before the three were summoned to the quarterdeck.

Standing near the massive wheel was a tall man in a black sea coat, skin almost as dark, with brass buckles, a leather tricorne casting shadow over his scarred face. His eyes were grey as sea stone, and his voice, when he spoke, carried like a rolling storm.

"I am Captain Greaves," he said. "This is my ship. I don't tolerate theft, mutiny, or dead weight. Earn your passage, keep to your duties, and don't ask questions about where we're headed. If you survive the journey, you'll walk away richer—or wiser."

Perched on a brass railing near the captain's shoulder was a Melborat— six-legged, with furless, mottled skin that shimmered in shifting hues. The creature flicked its narrow snout toward each of them, its skin turning a faint gray-blue.

"Don't mind Muzzle," Captain Greaves added, glancing at the creature. "He forecasts weather better than most sailors I've met."

Behind him, leaning against the rail with arms crossed, was someone they had seen before: Zarcan Lawnbar.

Ro narrowed her eyes.

"First Mate Lawnbar," Captain Greaves said without turning. "Keep them in line."

Zarcan gave a thin smile that didn't quite reach his eyes. "Wouldn't dream of anything less."

Seth murmured, "He's the First Mate now?"

"Looks like it," Zavalla replied under his breath. "This could be bad… or very, very bad."

As the Stormrider sailed farther from the safety of Melbonia and into the open sea, secrets began to stir beneath the surface —secrets in Ro's past, Zavalla's hope, Seth's destiny, and Milo's knowing glances.

And somewhere beyond the horizon, the Lost Island waited.

Chapter 16

Whisper of the Island

he *Stormrider* creaked and surged over rolling swells,

its bronze hull cutting clean through the green-blue sea. Above, the metal-and-lomek-hide sails shimmered with energy, catching winds that didn't always blow from the right direction. Below deck, the ship was alive with murmurs, labor, and the distant hiss of arcane engines that never quite went silent.

Seth had never been so far from land. From the deck's edge, the ocean stretched endless and unknowable, like a second sky. Zavalla stood beside him, watching the horizon as though it might blink back.

"We're in ancient waters," Zavalla murmured. "If the island's out there, it's hiding from the world."

Ro joined them, her face pale from salt air or worry. "How does one find a place that doesn't want to be found?"

Before either could answer, a bell rang out from the crow's nest.

"Ship spotted!" came the cry. "Two points to starboard!"

The *Stormrider's* crew stirred into motion. Captain Greaves barked orders while Zarcan—sharp-eyed and grim—directed the deckhands. The ship in question appeared not as a threat but as a wreck: a shattered vessel half-swallowed by the sea, its mast broken like a snapped twig, its figurehead scorched and blackened.

"A warning," Zarcan muttered, eyeing the floating ruin.

"Or a sign," Ro whispered.

Later, in the galley, Milo stirred a pot of strange green stew, glancing sideways at Ro. "*Stormrider* doesn't go this far out unless it's chasing something real," he said.

She frowned. "Like the Lost Island?"

He shrugged. "You didn't hear that from me."

Ro crossed her arms and leaned against the counter. "Is that stew supposed to be bubbling green? Or is that your signature style?"

Milo snorted. "It's called 'seaweed and shimmerroot stew.' Fancy name, terrible flavor."

"Comforting," Ro said dryly. "What's for dessert, saltwater pudding?"

He cracked a grin, flashing crooked teeth beneath a mop of red, curly hair. "Only on feast days. You want to stir this while I pretend to care about portion control?"

Ro stepped forward and took the spoon, pretending to take the job seriously. "Glad to know I've been promoted to assistant galley slave."

Milo raised an eyebrow. "You might be the only one on this ship I don't want to throw overboard yet."

"High praise," she said with a smirk.

They worked side by side for a time, exchanging sharp comments that softened into easier laughter. Ro noticed the way Milo moved around the kitchen—not gracefully, but with the confidence of someone who'd done it a hundred times. She handed him a ladle; he passed her a plate. There was rhythm to it.

As Ro leaned over to ladle out portions, Milo watched her more carefully.

"You know," he said after a moment, "you look familiar. Not from the taverns. Not from the docks. More like… something out of a painting."

Ro tensed. "I get that a lot."

He didn't press, only nodded. "Well, paintings lie. You've got more grit than brushstrokes."

A flicker of understanding passed between them. A small crack in the wall she'd built around her identity—and Milo had noticed.

Before they could speak further, the ship gave a lurch—just enough to remind them they were still sailing toward something vast and unknown.

When the crew gathered that night, it was under starlight and soft wind. Stories were shared in low tones—of islands that vanish, of sea creatures that sing sailors to sleep and drag them beneath the waves, of ancient machines buried under coral and kelp.

Zavalla listened with a stillness that seemed unnatural. Seth watched him closely, sensing something stirring in the old sorcerer's mind.

Finally, Zavalla spoke. "The Lost Island. It lies below sea level, hidden within a great chasm. The ocean pours into it like a waterfall from every side, masking it in mist and mystery."

Ro furrowed her brow. "Then how do we even see it?"

Zavalla raised his eyes to the stars. "From the sky. Only from above can the island be revealed. That's why it's remained hidden for so long. It's not lost—it's waiting. And not everyone who finds it is meant to."

The wind shifted. The ship's metal bones groaned softly as if reacting to his words.

As the *Stormrider* slipped into night, the horizon shivered—not with storm or swell, but something unseen. A presence. A whisper of magic older than memory. Somewhere below, wrapped in cascading water and ancient secrets, the Blue Dragon's treasure waited.

And it was watching them approach.

Chapter 17

Tides of Intent

eeks passed aboard the Stormrider, and the world of land faded into memory. The Beryldeep Sea—ancient, vast, and as changeable as thought—stretched in every direction. One day, it lay flat and reflective like hammered steel; the next, it rose in jagged waves that crashed against the bronze hull with an almost vengeful hunger. Time no longer ticked in hours but in sunrises, bruised skies, and the tightening of rope.

Clocks meant nothing here. Routine had become their measure: morning inspections, midday rationing, the hiss of arcane engines at night. Sea salt crusted every surface. Boots wore thin. Tempers, too.

Seth stood often at the bow, the wind tugging at his clothes, the pink gem on his shield glowing faintly with every change in the ship's rhythm. He was growing quieter, more aware—no longer a boy from Golden Arrow but something becoming.

Zavalla rarely spoke now, often lost in meditative silence, his gaze fixed at the horizon as though waiting for the sea to speak. He had begun sleeping less, the effort of watching for magical disturbances draining what little strength he had left. Yet sometimes, when alone, Zavalla's eyes flicked to the stormy skies with an intensity that suggested his thoughts were elsewhere—darker, deeper. At night, when the crew slept and the sea was calm, he would sit with his spellbook and stare at the constellation of dragonstones drawn on its worn pages. He never voiced the question aloud, but it echoed in his mind:

What if they were all brought together again? What could be rebuilt... or undone? It was a dangerous thought—and he knew it. But it was one he could never quite put down.

Occasionally, Zavalla would take Seth aside during quiet stretches of the journey. These lessons happened when the sea was calm and the crew distracted. On the rear deck or in the ship's hold, Zavalla would demonstrate the gentlest magics— glow spells, deflection wards, and the feel of elemental threads in the air.

"You don't command magic," Zavalla told him during one of their lessons, standing with his staff as Seth attempted to mimic his motions. "You court it. Entice it. Magic is like breath— natural, flowing—but it can choke you if taken too quickly."

Seth focused, his fingers forming the sigil for light. A small flicker sparked in his palm, then died with a hiss.

"Try again," Zavalla urged. "Let it come to you."

On the third attempt, the glow spell caught—a soft halo of pink light blooming between Seth's hands. It wasn't much, but it lingered longer than before. The gem on his shield pulsed in approval.

"Good," Zavalla said, though his voice was quieter than usual. "But remember what I told you. Magic may feel like a friend, but it doesn't forget your bloodline."

Seth looked at him. "Because of my mother."

Zavalla nodded. "And because of what you could become. Keep it in balance, or it will tip you."

Ro and Milo had formed an unlikely rhythm in the galley. Their banter, once sharp, had mellowed into a camaraderie that carried them through the long days. Milo, despite his usual grumbling, had begun cooking for the entire crew, slinging meals with surprising efficiency for someone his age. He took pride in his craft—even if it meant cursing at boiling pots and rogue fire-spirits. He now openly teased Ro, and she returned his jabs with a smirk or well-aimed spoonful of flour. Still, she caught him watching her sometimes, not with suspicion, but with wary recognition—as if he knew more than he let on.

Still, something festered beneath the calm.

Zarcan Lawnbar, officially the First Mate, prowled the decks like a wolf among sheep. His presence was shadow and steel, his gaze calculating. No one dared cross him. Some admired him. Most feared him. He had a way of appearing exactly where trouble might start, and a habit of finishing it before it could. Seth watched him carefully, unsure of the mercenary's true goals.

One night, while peeling shimmerroot in the flickering lamplight of the galley, Milo spoke in a low voice.

"You don't like him," Ro said.

Milo didn't look up. "Zarcan? He's got all the charm of a knife in the dark. You don't survive the things he has without losing something."

"He got us here," Ro offered, but her voice lacked conviction.

Milo met her eyes. "Yeah. But the question is why."

Above deck, the tension in the air grew thick. The clouds had turned heavy and strange, rolling in from every direction without wind. The crew grew restless. Even the arcane sails crackled with nervous energy.

100

Captain Greaves stepped onto the deck, his bootfalls echoing against the metal, his long coat snapping in the stiffening breeze. His weathered face was unreadable, but the twitch in his jaw betrayed unease.

Perched on his shoulder, nestled beneath his high collar, was Muzzle—the captain's Melborat. The furless, six-legged creature sniffed the air and blinked slowly, its narrow snout twitching. As it shifted in the captain's collar, its skin began to darken—first gray, then a slick, oily black with white jagged stripes.

"The wind's gone wrong," Greaves said in a low voice. "Something's waking beneath us."

From the crow's nest came a cry. "Swell rising! Eastward!"

But the sea didn't swell—it rose.

A wave, impossibly tall, built in the distance like a wall of water and wrath. The Beryldeep Sea had stirred from slumber. Rain came sideways, slicing through the rigging. Lightning arced across the clouds in silent threads of white fire.

Seth gripped the railing near the helm. Zavalla, eyes alight, whispered spells into the storm, trying to brace the ship against the heaving water. Ro and Milo were already above deck, struggling with ropes as wind tore at them. Milo's red curls plastered against his forehead as he shouted over the roar, "This stew better be worth it!"

Through the chaos, Zarcan remained unmoved. He stood at the prow, laughing—not madly, but like someone recognizing an old adversary. He and Greaves shouted orders in tandem, their voices cutting through the gale like twin blades.

And then the sea opened.

A trench, impossibly vast, yawning open below. The Beryldeep peeled away to reveal a chasm rimmed by waterfalls—ocean water pouring endlessly downward into darkness. It was not just a pit—it was a scar in the world.

Zavalla shouted, "That's it! The edge of the chasm—the island lies beneath!"

Captain Greaves barked, "Full sail! Brace for lift!"

Ro's eyes widened. "Lift? What does he mean—?"

The captain pointed to the rising wave. "We ride it—now!"

The Stormrider surged forward, arcane engines whining with sudden life. The massive wave loomed like a cliff, but Greaves showed no fear.

The ship struck the wave's base and climbed—higher, higher still—as if defying gravity itself. The hull shuddered. The sails flared. The roar of water was deafening. Seth braced himself, eyes wide.

Ro's foot slipped on the slick deck, and she fell sideways. Before she could hit the railing, Milo caught her with both arms.

"Careful," Milo said, catching her with both arms and steadying her on her feet.

Ro grumbled and grabbed the rail as the ship pitched again. "Thanks."

Milo gave a shrug. "Anytime."

Then they launched.

The Stormrider hurled skyward, using the wave as a ramp. The sea fell away, and the storm spun below like a broken wheel.

In the stunned silence that followed, the clouds parted.

Beneath the clearing sky, framed by sunlight and mist, hovered a sight none of them had expected:

An island—suspended within the heart of the storm, cradled above the trench by unknown forces. Water cascaded down its edges, pouring into the abyss below like silver threads. Vines curled along its cliffs. A single structure glimmered at its peak, an obsidian spire ringed with terraces and gardens clinging to impossible slopes.

Towering stone statues, half-buried in ivy, stood like forgotten guardians along the rim. Strange birds with crystalline wings circled above, shrieking in tones like bells.

Seth stared in awe. The air itself felt different—charged, ancient. Like the island was aware of them.

Zavalla's voice was hushed. "There it is… the Lost Island."

The storm had not hidden it. It had protected it.

And now, it waited.

They had found the island—but what lay upon it, or below it, was a mystery none of them were ready to face.

Chapter 18

The Descent

he *Stormrider* began its descent in a slow, cautious spiral, arcane thrusters firing in short bursts as the airship banked toward the island below. Captain Greaves leaned forward at the helm, eyes scanning the mist-shrouded terrain. "There," he pointed. "See that ridge? Half-buried tower, just east of the upper terraces. That structure looks intact—might offer shelter, maybe more."

The ancient building jutted from the stone like a broken tooth, its obsidian walls slick with moss but solid, untouched by the waterfalls cascading on all sides of the island. Overgrown stairways spiraled around it. The roof had caved in long ago, but the base was wide, stable, and half-sunken into a natural plateau—perfect cover from weather and prying eyes.

The captain turned toward the crew. "We'll set her down there. No sense lingering in the open."

The crew moved quickly. Sails retracted, stabilizers shifted, and the *Stormrider* hovered over the tower ruins before gently lowering onto the mossy ground with a hiss of escaping steam and a groan of old metal against ancient stone.

Captain Greaves gave quick orders. "Ground crew, stay with the ship. Secure her. Check for hull damage. I want full systems running by nightfall. If we're lucky, this structure might be defensible if we need it."

Seth and the others gathered at the lowered ramp, gazing out at the wild beauty of the island. The air felt dense—rich with the scent of damp earth and old magic. Ruined columns and shattered stone pathways spread out like veins beneath vines and creeping roots.

Milo stepped out last, thumping behind the others with a large blackened cooking pot snugly jammed on his head like a helmet. Ro turned and blinked. "Milo… what is that?"

He gave a dramatic shrug. "Emergency headgear. Might keep my brains from getting scrambled out here. Also, keeps the rain off."

Seth burst into laughter. Ro followed, shaking her head with a smirk. "You're ridiculous."

"Yeah, but I'm fully seasoned for battle," Milo replied, and gave the pot a proud tap. "Just in case anyone tries to stir up trouble."

From that moment on, Milo began slipping food puns into conversation whenever possible. As they moved supplies from the ship, he warned them to "stay saucy" and muttered that the ruins looked "half-baked." Ro groaned at each one, but Seth seemed to enjoy the levity.

Still, something deeper hummed beneath the island's strange calm.

Zavalla remained quiet, his eyes fixed on the horizon—but his fingers twitched slightly at his side, like they remembered spells of warning long forgotten.

Zarcan Lawnbar stood apart, feigning disinterest. In truth, his heart pounded in his chest. The building they landed on matched the sketches etched in the corner of his map. He felt

the worn parchment tucked into his coat press against his ribs
—a secret guide to the heart of the island's true treasure. He'd
told Greaves only of other possible ruins, artifacts, relics.
Enough to convince the captain. Not enough to share the prize.

Soon, he thought. Soon, I'll find it.

As the crew began unloading supplies and setting up a
temporary camp within the tower ruins, the adventuring party
descended the ramp, stepping onto stone that had not felt a
living footfall in centuries.

Ro chuckled. "Stick with me, cook. We'll keep each other
alive."

The island didn't just feel alive—it felt aware. Zavalla stepped
off last, his eyes lingering not on the ruins or jungle, but on the
amulet still glowing in Ro's hand. There was a calculation
behind his gaze.

As the jungle swallowed them in green shadow, the true test of
their journey was just beginning.

The ruins of the tower provided eerie shelter. Moss-covered
stones and shattered archways whispered of a civilization long
lost to time. Vines hung from the crumbled ceiling like sleeping
serpents, and strange runes were etched along the interior walls
—some still faintly glowing with forgotten meaning.

Seth stood near the entrance with Ro, Milo, Zavalla, and
Ember—who perched on a fallen pillar, her scaled wings
folded tight, eyes scanning every corner with alert curiosity.
She let out a soft, rumbling chirp, tail flicking like a cat's.

"I think she's nervous," Ro whispered.

"Or she smells something we can't," Seth replied. "She always gets twitchy when there's magic nearby."

Milo adjusted the dented cooking pot he'd strapped to his head. "Maybe she just doesn't trust my cooking. Not every stew needs dragonfruit, you know."

Seth laughed, and Ro gave him a sideways grin. "If you start speaking in stew recipes, I'm leaving you behind."

"Only the finest puns on this expedition," Milo said, adopting a mock-chef tone. "Hope you're hungry for danger."

Ember blinked once, unimpressed, and fluttered briefly before settling on Zavalla's shoulder.

By midday, the group gathered to make a plan. Ro traced their position on a roughly sketched map from the captain, the amulet in her hand pulsing ever so faintly. Ember crept closer to investigate the glowing artifact, snorting as if she could sense something in its magic.

"The amulet's tugging east," Ro said, nodding toward the jagged cliffs that rose beyond the ruin. "If the blue gem is anywhere, it's that direction."

Seth nodded. "Then that's where we start. We'll scout a path before it gets too late. Quiet, careful, and we stick together."

Milo tapped the pot on his head. "Unless you want lunch before we go, then I lead."

Zavalla chuckled softly but didn't offer one of his usual warnings or riddles. Instead, he leaned on his staff, Ember occasionally nudging his arm curiously. He reached over and scratched her head gently. "She's grown more alert latelyand bigger."

107

"She's always been smart," Seth said. "But lately, it feels like she's... sensing more."

From the shadows of the broken archway, a familiar voice interrupted the calm.

"Going on a treasure hunt without me?" Zarcan Lawnbar strolled into the open with a lazy confidence. Behind him stood five crew members—rougher-looking than most, some with faded red sashes or shirts woven into their gear, a weathered contrast to the jungle around them.

Seth's eyes narrowed. "You're leading a separate party?"

Zar gave a shallow nod. "Captain's orders. The island's too large to comb through with just one group. I hand-picked a few of the more experienced hands."

Ro glanced between the groups, noting the mix of personalities and the odd flashes of red in their clothing. She leaned toward Seth with a crooked smile. "Here's hoping red doesn't mean first to vanish. I'd hate to be a walking omen."

Captain Greaves followed them in, arms crossed. "It's a split expedition. We search the island in sections and regroup before nightfall."

"It's already noon," Ro pointed out. "That doesn't give us long."

"Long enough," the captain said. "We aren't spending a night out there unless we absolutely have to."

Zarcan's grin didn't reach his eyes. "We'll take the aqueduct trail to the cliffs. Old stonework usually hides more than just water."

Before setting out, Zar divided the crew into three search parties. He led one group himself, and Captain Greaves assigned Seth, Ro, Zavalla, Milo, and Ember to another, accompanied by three other crewmates. The third group, composed of the remaining sailors, was tasked with checking the shoreline and nearby ruins. Some of the sailors wore red sashes, shirts, or bandanas—accidental or perhaps just coincidence—but Ro's gaze lingered on them all the same.

The groups began gathering their supplies. Ro checked their map and adjusted her belt, while Milo packed rations into a canvas sack, mumbling about "jungle stew with a side of disaster." Ember fluttered down and tapped her snout on Milo's cooking pot helmet, then mimicked wearing it by hunching her wings around her head. Seth and Ro burst into laughter.

"That's it," Milo said, smirking. "Even the dragon thinks I'm a joke."

"She thinks you're delicious," Ro quipped.

Ember gave a low, amused chirp.

Zavalla watched them quietly, his staff pressed lightly into the mossy floor. He seemed distracted, gaze flicking occasionally toward the forest. As the others prepared, he stepped over to Seth.

"There may be wards left behind by whoever lived here," he said quietly. "Old magic. It may react to us."

Seth nodded. "Anything we should avoid?"

"Everything, until we understand it." Zavalla glanced at the ruins one last time. "These stones weren't just for shelter. They meant something. Places like this remember."

Ro rejoined them with Ember in tow. "Let's move before the other groups get too far. The sooner we find something, the better our chances of getting out of here before nightfall."

The expedition moved out, weaving through mossy underbrush and into the dense heart of the island. High above, broken shafts of sunlight pierced the thick canopy, painting everything in green-gold hues. Strange bird calls echoed in the distance, and the air was thick with moisture and mystery.

High above the island, sun streamed through broken clouds, casting shifting light through the jungle canopy. Somewhere deeper in the wilderness, Zarcan moved with purpose—his own map hidden beneath his coat, and his mind already several steps ahead of everyone else.

He didn't need to find the blue gem.

He already knew where it was.

Chapter 19

The Jungle Watches

ungle heat swelled beneath the canopy, trapping the party in a haze of humidity and the thick perfume of wild vegetation. Towering trees stretched like pillars toward the sky, their trunks wrapped in the spindly limbs of Zime Vines. Dew from Numbal Flowers glistened in the underbrush, while strange birdcalls echoed above—haunting trills that sounded almost too coordinated to be natural.

The ruins loomed ahead. Crumbling archways and weather-worn statues jutted from the earth like teeth, half-swallowed by the jungle. Most were humanoid in shape, but their features were curious—graceful, with finely sculpted faces and sharp, intelligent eyes.

Ro stepped cautiously through a broken colonnade, her eyes scanning the carved visages. "They almost look like Ebilites," she said slowly. "But older. Regal."

Zavalla ran a hand over a nearby pillar. "It's strange to see them in a place like this. These statues are remarkably well preserved."

"Menacus was supposed to be their homeland, right?" Seth said, glancing at another stone figure. "But it was destroyed."

"Maybe it didn't get destroyed," Ro murmured. "Maybe it sank —and this is what's left."

The group continued, winding through twisted roots and stone remnants, until Seth suddenly knelt beside the trail.

"Look at this." He lifted a lumpy, yellowish fruit with a dark red base. It had clearly been bitten into—jagged marks still fresh along the flesh.

"Jooblin," Milo said, leaning in with a frown. "Raw. Bitter as sin. Only Ebilites eat it like this."

Ro wrinkled her nose. "Makes my tongue curl just thinking about it."

"Which means Ebilites are nearby," Zavalla added, lowering his voice.

As they moved on, Milo suddenly yelped and swatted at his neck.

"Ugh, what was—"

Zavalla grabbed his shoulder and turned him. "Did it sting you?"

"I don't think so. I felt something, but it just grazed—"

"Folosis Fly," Zavalla muttered grimly, examining a smear of green ichor on Milo's collar. "If it had stung you, you'd be dead already."

"That's... comforting," Milo said, pale.

Not far ahead, a sharp cry rang out. One of the crew, dressed in a faded red shirt, stumbled from the brush, clutching his shoulder. He didn't speak—he couldn't. Foam lined his mouth as his knees buckled beneath him.

Ro and Seth ran to him, but it was too late. Zavalla knelt, checking the man's pulse, then shook his head.

"Poisoned," he said. "Folosis. No time to treat it. He was dead the second it struck."

Ember, wings half-raised, growled low and circled the air above them.

They buried the man beneath a grove of Tokoon palms, each tall stalk capped with dense, leafy fronds. Clusters of dark purple fruit, shaped like tight, bush-like fists, dangled beneath the leaves—Tokoon, a salty, nutritious staple across Acklelend. Though poisonous to Lopkins, it was a common and hardy jungle crop, thriving in the moist, fertile soil here.

Milo knelt beneath one of the trees and plucked a bulbous fruit from its stem.

"Hey," he said, rubbing it between his fingers. "If we mix Tokoon with Jooblin... it might mask the bitterness. Worth trying."

"You want to cook it?" Ro asked skeptically.

"No time," he said, slicing both fruits open with his belt knife. "Chew fast. It'll taste like swamp water and regret, but it might keep your face from melting."

Ro sighed. "Fine. But if I throw up, I'm aiming for your boots."

The jungle offered no peace. Insects droned, and something—someone—watched from the trees.

Ro kept her hand near her weapon.

"We're not alone," she said.

Seth nodded. "Let's keep moving."

Beneath the canopy, ancient secrets waited—and the deeper they went, the more the island began to whisper. Not with words, but with rustling branches and the quiet crunch of unseen footsteps not their own.

Chapter 20

Signs and Shadows

The deeper they pushed into the jungle, the stranger the terrain became. Trees widened into towering columns with bark like cracked leather, and thick branches wove overhead to form a living canopy that dimmed the sunlight into scattered green shafts. The ruins grew denser, too—crumbled staircases overgrown with moss, shattered temples with doorways swallowed by roots, and half-sunken courtyards filled with broken statuary.

Despite the wildness, there was order—paths that felt too straight to be natural, stones deliberately laid, and vines trimmed away in places as if by unseen hands.

"They've been maintaining this," Ro whispered, running her fingers along a cleared trail. "Someone still lives here."

Ember growled low, her pupils narrowing as she scanned the tree line.

They weren't alone.

Zavalla paused at a mossy archway, his staff tapping lightly on the stone. "There's old magic here. Sleeping, but close to waking."

"Do we go around?" Seth asked.

"No," Zavalla said, then added after a breath, "We go through. But carefully."

They entered the ruined structure—an old atrium, by the looks of it. Sunlight filtered through the cracked ceiling. Vines hung like curtains. Strange markings lined the walls—glyphs older than any language Ro had studied. Some glowed faintly in the dark.

Zavalla muttered, "Ebilite script. Older dialect, I think."

"You can read it?" Milo asked.

"Enough to be uneasy."

As they crossed the chamber, a sound echoed from deeper within: the unmistakable rustle of movement. Something was watching them—again.

Ro's fingers tightened around the hilt of her blade.

And then they saw it.

At the far edge of the atrium, half-hidden behind a collapsed pillar, stood a figure no taller than Ro's shoulder. Skin the color of wild honey. Large, intelligent eyes. Hair woven with feathers and bark. A simple spear in hand.

An Ebilite—but not like the ones who lived on the mainland.

This one was wilder. More primal. Dressed in bark and animal hide, painted in swirls of plant dyes, yet standing with unmistakable poise and awareness. The Ebilite stared at them —unafraid, unblinking.

Zavalla raised a hand slowly. "We mean no harm."

The Ebilite didn't speak. It simply vanished behind the stone.

"Did… did it just disappear?" Milo whispered.

"No," Seth said. "It moved. Fast."

Ro knelt and picked something up from where the Ebilite had stood—a piece of carved bone strung on twine, shaped like a spiral shell. A pendant.

"They wanted us to see them," she said.

Zavalla's brow furrowed. "Or they're testing us."

From deeper in the jungle, a horn sounded—deep and resonant, like a conch being blown.

It wasn't a warning.

It was a summons.

It happened fast.

No sooner had the group stepped through the atrium at the heart of the island—past vines clinging to sunken walls, past old stone steps overgrown with moss—than the trap was triggered.

At the far edge of the atrium, the stone gave a deceptive shimmer, just a few feet before what looked like a sealed inner chamber. But the moment Seth stepped forward, the ground collapsed.

A hidden pit trap swallowed them whole.

Before he could even raise his shield, they were plunging into cold, dark water.

117

When Seth opened his eyes, coral light flickered through the deep. Strange, twisting vines swayed in the current, their leaves glowing with pulsing bioluminescence. A shimmering bubble enclosed them, allowing them to breathe—but not escape. Magical currents dragged them downward through a spiraling tunnel of translucent stone.

They emerged in a vast, underwater cavern, carved from coral and volcanic glass, dimly lit by the eerie glow of deep-sea plants. Guarding the chamber were the Ebilites—small, elegant beings about four feet tall, with sharply pointed ears, luminous eyes, and delicate features. Their skin shimmered with pearlescent tones, and their clothes were woven from coral fibers and sea-silk. They looked like a strange cross between elves and deep-sea fairies, but their eyes were wary, hardened by a culture of secrecy and survival.

Seth, Ro, Zavalla, Ember, and Milo were unarmed, surrounded, and caged by woven kelp bars reinforced with glowing barnacle runes.

The Ebilites spoke in hissing tones, their language full of clicks and rippling pulses. It was unintelligible—until Zavalla muttered something and waved his hand in a subtle circle. A ripple of magic passed through the group, and suddenly the hissing resolved into comprehensible words.

"Outsiders," one of the Ebilites said, his voice cold and formal. He wore a mantle of dark sea-leaves and a helm of translucent shell. His gaze lingered on Ro's cloak, sensing the Amnathoth Amulet hidden beneath it. "You trespass on sacred ground. The deep sings of foreign blood and the stirring of ancient things."

They were dragged into a cell shaped like a spiraled nautilus shell. A strange seaweed on the floor gave off a calming mist— probably to keep prisoners docile. Ember growled low, her small form pacing in agitation.

118

Milo, always quick to adapt, spoke up as the guards left. "Anyone else notice our hosts are hungry? I caught a whiff of dried urchin stew on one of them. Bet I could outcook their best with one claw tied behind my back."

Ro laughed softly, more from nerves than humor.

Later, Milo managed to barter with one of the guards—offering a perfectly roasted swamp root dish using sea herbs and Ember's residual fire heat. The guard accepted, and returned later with fresh water and softer sleeping moss. Small wins.

That night, in the dim glow of the cavern walls, Ro and Seth sat side by side.

She leaned close, whispering, "You handled that fall better than most."

Seth smiled faintly. "It helps when you've been falling for days."

Their eyes met, and something unspoken passed between them. A quiet moment, fragile but real.

Nearby, Zavalla sat with his back against the coral bars, silent. He watched the others with narrowed eyes, but his attention was fixed inward. He could feel something—resonance, yes— but not from possession. From nearness. The Blue Treasure was close. He could sense it, like a distant melody that tugged at the edge of his thoughts.

But he said nothing.

The group didn't know how long they would be kept prisoner —or what trials lay ahead—but they knew one thing: the treasure was on this island.

And the Ebilites were not the only ones guarding it.

Chapter 21

Trial of the Coral Throne

he next morning beneath the island passed in a blur of flickering lights, ancient chants, and murmured warnings from the Ebilite guards who monitored their every movement. The Ebilites returned—not with food this time, but with judgment in their hands and intent in their eyes.

"You have trespassed upon sacred ground," intoned the same elder who had first spoken to them, his voice echoing through the shell-like chamber like waves crashing against coral cliffs. "But the sea does not judge on entry alone. There is a rite, a trial. If you pass it, you may walk freely—though not without our eyes upon you."

"And if we fail?" Ro asked, her arms crossed, voice steady but sharp.

The elder's pale, glistening gaze turned toward her. "Then the deep keeps what the deep is owed."

They were escorted from the nautilus cell into a massive amphitheater-like cavern, hollowed from coral and obsidian stone. The ceiling stretched so high it vanished into blue mist, and the walls were carved with images of sea beasts, ancient battles, and swirling water spirits. Bioluminescent anemones pulsed softly like ceremonial torches along the steps. At the center of the cavern stood a throne made of woven pink coral and stone kelp, raised on a dais surrounded by a shallow pool that shimmered with luminous tides.

"The Trial of the Coral Throne," one of the guards whispered. "Face your truths. Face your fears."

Ro exchanged a tense glance with Seth. "Let's hope our truths don't get us drowned."

Zavalla stepped forward slowly, his eyes tracing the arcane symbols carved into the walls. "This is not a test of strength, but of soul."

One by one, the group stepped into the pool surrounding the throne. The water rose to their ankles and began to swirl unnaturally. When it reached their knees, a strange pull yanked them forward—gently but unyielding—and then down. The glowing tide wrapped around them like fingers of light and dragged them into visions.

The Trial had begun.

Milo found himself in the heart of a bustling kitchen, lanterns swaying and pots boiling over roaring fires. The air brimmed with the smell of garlic, peppercorn, and fried clams. Chaos moved around him—cooks shouting, steam rising—and then came the voice.

His father stepped in, arms folded, frowning. "Still burning onions, boy? You'll never earn your name with boiled roots."

Milo, breath shallow, stepped away from the counter and wiped his brow. But instead of shrinking, he met his father's gaze. "Maybe not your name. But I'm building mine. And I help people—more than you ever did."

The kitchen began to blur, melting into golden mist.

Ro stood on a marble floor under chandeliers that glittered like constellations. Silk-robed nobles spun in dance, their laughter echoing like hollow bells. At the far end, her father stood near the dais, arm draped around the nobleman she'd been promised to. His voice boomed like iron striking stone. "Duty before desire. You will marry, and you will obey."

In her hand was a mask—elegant and heavy.

She stared at it, then dropped it to the floor and stepped on it with deliberate grace. "My future belongs to me."

The ballroom shattered like crystal.

Seth stood atop the cliffs overlooking Golden Arrow. Below, flames tore through the valley. Smoke and screams rose into the night. On the edge of the cliff stood a boy—his younger self—watching it all unfold with tears on his cheeks.

"We can't save her," the boy whispered.

Seth looked at the shield in his hands. Its pink stone glowed faintly.

He knelt beside the boy and pressed the shield into his arms. "Then save what you can. Protect others. That's what matters."

The boy nodded. The fire receded.

Zavalla stood alone in a forest made of frozen obsidian trees. Shadows moved at the edges—specters of those he'd failed. Bobooshkin appeared at the edge of the clearing, holding the Flaming Sword. Snow fell like ash.

"You thought power could redeem your past," Bobooshkin said.

123

Zavalla stared at him, grief written into every line of his face. "No. I thought it could protect those who still had a future. I was wrong."

The sword cracked into a thousand shards of red glass. Zavalla closed his eyes, breathing in the cold.

When the water released them, they surfaced with gasps, collapsing onto the coral steps. Though their clothes were dry, their skin was slick with cold sweat. Their expressions were different—older, perhaps. Marked.

But not all of them emerged.

Two other crew members—Merro and Jath—were pulled from the pool unconscious. Their trials had overcome them. The Ebilites laid them gently aside, eyes solemn.

"They were not ready," the elder said. "The sea does not drown without reason. They will wake, but changed."

The Ebilite elder turned toward the others and surveyed them carefully.

"You have passed. Not by strength, but by recognition. The sea sees you now. And it does not forget."

As they were led back toward the upper caverns, a younger Ebilite lingered behind to speak. "Other groups came also. They uncovered golden relics in the west and broke sacred stones. They roused things that sleep."

Ro's jaw tightened. "Zar. That has to be him."

Seth nodded grimly. "He's not just looting. He's tearing the island apart."

124

Once back in their quarters, they were granted a rare courtesy: food, water, and time to rest. Milo roasted what was left of his smoked river crabs using a heated coral plate, and Ember, whose appetite had begun shifting again, devoured them with gusto.

Her body had changed. Her tail was longer. Her wings had thickened. Even her stare had grown sharper, more focused. She no longer moved with the kittenish clumsiness of a hatchling—there was grace now, and purpose.

"She's definitely growing," Ro said, watching Ember stretch her limbs with slow, careful movement.

"She's always liked my cooking," Milo said proudly. "I make dragons thrive."

Seth chuckled, settling beside Ember and running his hand along her back. She trilled in contentment, nestling closer.

"She'll outgrow my shoulder soon," he murmured. "Probably eat twice what I do by the next moon."

That night, the group sat in a loose circle, surrounded by the soft pulsing lights of the cavern walls. No words were needed. The silence between them felt earned. They had faced more than riddles and trials—they had glimpsed their own reflections and survived.

The Blue Treasure was near. They could feel it.

And now, they had permission to seek it—and something more valuable still: a shared resolve.

Chapter 22

Temple of the Deep Crown

ist clung low over the island's jagged heart as the

group pressed deeper toward its center. A jagged ridge of coral stone rose before them, like the fractured spine of some ancient sea-beast. According to the Ebilite map—etched into living kelp and gifted to them in solemn ceremony—the temple of the Aquarian Crown lay just beyond.

The jungle of the island gave way to uneven stone, blackened by salt and time. Strange shell-like towers rose around them, hollow and ringed with runes in a language none of them could read. The wind that rustled through them carried a low moan, like the breath of sleeping titans. But they all felt it.

Power.

The very air buzzed with quiet pressure, as if something immense and invisible were coiled just out of sight, watching, waiting.

The submerged temple finally revealed itself as they crested a hilltop overlooking an inland lagoon. At the center of the water sat a massive circular platform, partially submerged, shaped like a curling nautilus. Its outer walls were carved with immense dragons—coiled and sleeping—each inlaid with sapphire glass and deep cerulean stone that glittered like trapped ocean light. A narrow, algae-covered bridge led to the structure's outer rim, just above the waterline.

"It's beautiful," Ro whispered, her voice laced with awe—and unease.

Zavalla confirmed. "This temple predates the Loopkin collapse."

As they approached, Ember shifted restlessly at Seth's side, her wings flaring slightly. She sniffed the air and let out a low rumble, sensing something they couldn't. Her scales shimmered faintly in the growing humidity.

Two of the crew members who had accompanied them—Merro and Jath—trailed behind, still shaken. They hadn't passed the Trial of the Coral Throne. The Ebilites had declared their hearts clouded with selfishness. They were allowed to travel on, but forbidden to touch any relics within the temple. Their steps were hesitant, and their eyes never strayed far from the shadows.

Merro eyed the stonework uneasily. "You sure this place won't collapse on us?"

Zavalla gave him a look. "Only if your conscience is heavy enough."

Inside the outer ring of the temple, they descended a series of slick steps into the cool blue interior. The walls shimmered with trapped air pockets and living coral veins. Faint bioluminescence pulsed through the stone. At the center of the room, surrounded by a spiral of aqueducts and cracked tile, was a massive circular disk embedded in the floor. Symbols rotated across its surface like the hands of a clock—except they didn't mark time.

127

"This is the mechanism," Seth said, crouching beside the device. "There has to be a pattern. Something that'll open the way."

Ro knelt next to him, her rogue instincts flaring. Her fingers moved lightly over the grooves and symbols, tracing their sequence with practiced ease. "These runes repeat—here, here, and again here. It's not just a puzzle… it's a trap."

She paused, then shifted one of the disks with a deliberate click. "There. That one resets the others. It's like a fail-safe. Whoever built this didn't just want to keep people out—they wanted to test them."

"You really know your locks," Seth muttered.

Ro smirked. "Steal enough noble vaults, you get a feel for the ancient stuff."

Zavalla nodded. "Or a lock," he said, watching the walls.

Together, they began manipulating the disks under Ro's direction. Each disk turned with a sound like stone weeping. Water spilled down from carved channels, flowing faster with each correct turn. The chamber responded with creaks and groans, as if it resented being awakened.

"What if we flood the chamber?" Ro asked, glancing nervously at the rising tide.

"Then we hope we're fast swimmers," Milo muttered, adjusting his satchel and gripping a nearby column.

Ember darted ahead, her tail sweeping over a section of the floor. The stone beneath her glowed. Seth rushed over and activated the final symbol. The mechanism locked into place with a heavy grind—and the entire floor began to descend.

The group held their breath as the platform groaned and began its descent, the water surging around them like a living thing. Light refracted strangely through the walls, casting dancing shadows of sea creatures that weren't really there.

The platform passed beneath the surface until they emerged in a massive dome of dry air far below the lagoon. The silence here was ancient and deep, like a temple submerged in time.

The chamber shimmered like the inside of a pearl. At its center stood a pedestal of coral and light, its surface gently pulsing with internal rhythm.

And resting upon it—the Aquarian Crown.

It was forged of silver-blue filigree, shaped like a cresting wave, its center set with a teardrop-shaped blue gem that pulsed like a heartbeat.

They approached slowly, reverently. Even Milo seemed speechless.

Ro reached for Seth's arm. "Wait. Something's wrong."

He met her gaze, trying to reassure her. "We've come this far. We're not turning back now."

Zavalla stepped forward beside them. His voice was quiet but carried an eerie weight.

"The Blue Crown does not answer to ambition," Zavalla said quietly. "It was forged for those who serve, not rule—for hearts that give before they take."

Seth stared at the crown.

He could feel it watching… Waiting.

Chapter 23

The Crown's Trap

he temple groaned as ancient gears churned beneath the group's feet, awakened after centuries of slumber. The sound was deep and guttural, like a beast long buried and stirred from its dreamless sleep. The coral walls trembled, water sloshing through shifting stone channels, cascading down walls where glowing moss had bloomed in peace for a thousand years. The final mechanism clicked into place with a thunderous clunk, and the sound echoed like a war drum through the chamber.

A low rumble rolled through the sanctum, vibrating the air itself. Slowly, methodically, the water began to drain, pulled away by unseen channels beneath their feet. What had once been a serene lagoon transformed into a swirling vortex of motion. The floor beneath them revealed its true shape—a massive circular platform encrusted in white coral and blue crystal veins that pulsed with light. At its center, rising like a delicate bloom, stood a pedestal shaped like a sea lily.

Upon that pedestal rested the Aquarian Crown.

It glowed softly in the dim chamber, a circlet of seafoam-silver and glistening sapphire. Despite its delicate appearance, the crown radiated ancient power. The blue gem at its center pulsed like a heartbeat, and tiny droplets of condensation rolled off its edges like tears mourning something long lost.

Seth stepped forward, breath shallow, eyes fixed on the relic. It felt as though the weight of the ocean pressed down on him, yet he could not look away. His footsteps echoed softly on the slick coral floor.

Ro's voice, soft but sharp, cut through the silence. "Careful. It might be trapped."

Zavalla narrowed his eyes, scanning the room with quiet suspicion. "Everything in this place is."

Still, Seth reached out. As his fingertips brushed the cool metal of the crown, a tremor ripped through the chamber.

The ground beneath them lurched. The pedestal hissed as it sank back into the floor, vanishing with the sharp clatter of shifting stone. From somewhere far above, a deep metallic thud shook the coral-laced ceiling.

Then, the island began to rise.

"The island's surfacing!" Milo shouted, scrambling backward, eyes wide with panic.

"Move!" Ro shouted. "Back to the ship—now!"

They bolted. Their footsteps slapped against wet stone as they tore down the now-drying passageways. Alarms began to sound from the heart of the temple—an eerie chorus of melodic chimes, grinding gears, and the roar of rushing water. Light streamed through cracks in the walls as the structure groaned and shifted around them.

Seth clutched the crown to his chest as they ran, his legs aching, lungs burning. Every heartbeat felt like it echoed the pulse of the crown itself. Behind them, the corridor trembled and sprayed mist into the air as seawater reversed direction, pulled away by the ancient mechanism that was forcing the island to the surface.

They reached the final chamber before the exit when a deafening pop filled the air—followed by a hiss. Smoke erupted from the archway ahead, thick and acrid. It poured into the corridor like an invading stormcloud, choking the light.

"Get back!" Zavalla growled, drawing energy into his palm, but it was too late.

Shadows flickered within the fog. A curved blade flashed. A shape darted forward—quick and violent.

Zar emerged like a ghost from the haze, his face wrapped in soaked bandages, his boots dripping with seawater, and his eyes burning with determination.

"Thanks for doing the hard part," he hissed.

Seth didn't even get a chance to raise the crown. Zar struck fast, slamming into him with brutal force. The crown slipped from Seth's grasp and skittered across the stone floor, catching a glint of unnatural light as it rolled.

Zar snatched it in one smooth motion, turned, and vanished back into the mist.

"No!" Seth cried, stumbling after him, but Ro caught his arm.

"Wait! Look!" she shouted.

Behind them, the walls cracked. A tremendous groan echoed through the chamber as the water surged back in—no longer gentle, but ravenous. It came crashing down the corridor, a serpent of foam and fury, devouring the air with its roar.

132

"We'll drown if we stay!" Ro shouted.

There was no time to argue. Hearts pounding, breath ragged, they turned and fled. The sound of the flood behind them was deafening, a thunderous pursuit that rattled the very walls. Coral cracked and shattered beneath their boots, and the air thickened with rising heat and steam pouring from fractured vents.

They sprinted through the final tunnel just as the sea exploded upward through the ruined passage, blasting sunlight into the corridor like a divine reprieve. The ground beneath them gave one last lurch as the island surfaced with a surge, waves crashing outward and rolling across the exposed stone.

They collapsed onto the wet cobblestone, coughing, soaked, and breathless. The air was thick with salt and panic. Behind them, the temple stood silent once more—but it was no longer a place of reverence. It had become a trap, reset and ready to lure the next souls who dared seek its secrets.

The Aquarian Crown was gone.

Zar had vanished into the mist, the crown in hand.

.

Zar had won—*for now.*

Chapter 24

Treachery at Sea

The Stormrider sat anchored high within the hollow ruins of a broken coral tower, balanced on ancient stone above a rising tide. The ship creaked, her hull straining as the waters below surged with growing unrest. Aboard her, the crew watched the horizon and the ruins in tense silence, hands on ropes and weapons, their breaths shallow with anticipation.

From below, a geyser of seawater exploded from the temple's entrance. A moment later, Seth, Ro, Zavalla, Milo, and Ember stumbled from the mist, soaked and battered. Their eyes locked on the Stormrider perched high above, unreachable by normal means.

"We'll never climb fast enough," Ro said, panting.

"Then we climb what we can," Seth growled. "Ember—stay close."

With Ember's help, the group scaled the coral-encrusted ruins. Sharp edges bit into their hands, and the stone flaked beneath their boots, but they pushed onward. The crew above lowered rope ladders and hauled them aboard one by one. As soon as the last of them crossed the rail, Captain Greaves barked his command.

"Raise the sails! Ready the ballistae! The sea's not done with us yet!"

Sails snapped open, and the Stormrider lurched into motion. The island rumbled behind them, but something far worse approached.

A silence fell. Wind died. Waves stilled. The sea became a breath held.

Then, from behind a jagged reef, a shadow emerged—a sleek, black vessel with serpent-carved rails and sails as dark as the abyss. It glided forward like a predator. On the quarterdeck, Zar stood cloaked in storm, the Aquarian Crown glowing faintly on his brow.

He raised his hand.

The sea exploded.

Waves rose like walls. Wind screamed. Lightning tore the sky as rain fell in sheets. Stormclouds twisted into a vortex above Zar's ship, casting it in writhing shadow.

"He's wielding the crown!" Milo yelled.

Zar's ship surged forward, faster than any wind should allow. Harpoons launched, thudding into the Stormrider's hull. Arcane blasts followed, raining destruction across the deck. Crew members dove for cover as the storm intensified.

"Fire all weapons!" Greaves commanded. "Target their helm and rigging!"

Crossbows and ballistae loosed a volley, bolts trailing fire and lightning. Ro and Seth worked in tandem, covering the deck and calling out targets. Ember soared through the storm, dodging lightning and lashing winds to drop flame on the enemy vessel.

Zavalla stood firm at the bow, staff raised, chanting over the howling gale. A shimmering barrier shielded the Stormrider briefly—but a lance of water-magic pierced the veil and struck him squarely. He flew backward and crumpled.

"Zavalla!" Ro screamed, crawling across the slick deck toward him.

Seth's fury boiled over. "Ember!" he called, pointing toward Zar's ship.

Ember banked hard and breathed a gout of flame to cover Seth's path. Seizing the moment, Seth sprinted across the deck and climbed onto the rigging. With a sharp tug, he released one of the cargo lines tied to a crossbeam above—its coil snapping taut in the storm winds. Using the tension like a slingshot, he swung outward into the air, hurtling across the chasm of sea. He landed hard on Zar's deck, sword drawn.

Zar met him, the crown flickering. "Back again?" he sneered.

Seth raised his shield, and the rose heart-gem at its center pulsed with radiant energy. As he closed the distance, he whispered a focus phrase Zavalla had taught him—just enough to ripple the air around Zar in a sharp burst of light and static. It wasn't a powerful spell, but it disrupted Zar's stance, buying Seth a split-second advantage. He needed every edge he could get.

Their clash echoed through the storm. Zar's strikes were fierce and unrelenting—each movement backed not just by training, but by the raw elemental force of the Aquarian Crown. He moved with precision, his blade cutting through wind and rain with unnatural grace, water magic lashing from his free hand in sweeping arcs. Seth gritted his teeth, doing everything he could to stay on the defensive, using the shield to deflect blow after blow and redirect the brunt of Zar's magical assaults. When a whip of seawater lashed toward him, he instinctively thrust the shield forward. A pink wave of light burst outward, disrupting the arcane torrent.

He ducked beneath a spinning strike and responded with a sweeping kick, knocking Zar off-balance.

Water coiled around Zar like a serpent, lashing out in blades. Seth sidestepped and used the shield again, creating a shockwave that dispersed the nearest magic. He wasn't as strong, or as skilled—but the crown's power had made Zar overconfident.

With every move, Seth mixed swordplay with bursts of instinctive magic—brief pulses of force, flickers of radiant light, and subtle shifts in the air that bent Zar's strikes a hair off-target. He was beginning to feel the rhythm of battle—not through skill alone, but through the faint hum of power awakened inside him. Each deflection, each counterstrike, grew sharper, steadier, guided by something deeper than training. Sparks flew as their blades clashed. Seth landed a heavy blow to Zar's side, and the crown wavered on his head.

A massive wave rose behind them. Seth ducked beneath Zar's swing, rammed his shoulder forward, and knocked the man sprawling. The crown flew.

It clattered across the deck.

Seth dove, rolled, and reached for the crown—just as Ember swept low across the deck. Her talons flashed, snatching the Aquarian Crown in a precise, practiced motion before it could tumble into the sea.

"Go!" Seth shouted, waving her off.

Ember beat her wings and soared skyward through the storm, the crown clutched tight.

Zar screamed in rage, lunging after her, but Seth slammed into him with the full weight of his momentum, driving him back into the collapsing deck.

With the crown secured and Zar momentarily stunned, Seth scanned the chaos for a way off the burning ship. He spotted a fallen mast straining against a tangled mess of rigging and sails —its rope still tethered to a higher spar. Without hesitation, Seth slashed the tensioned rope and grabbed hold as it recoiled, launching himself skyward in a swinging arc over the ravaged sea.

Rain battered his face. Fire licked at the edges of the sailcloth. Below, debris floated like shattered bones. As the Stormrider veered nearby, Seth angled his body and let go—crashing hard onto the deck, tumbling across the planks.

He rolled to his knees, soaked and gasping.

Ro and Milo crouched over Zavalla, who stirred with a groan.

"You made it," Zavalla rasped.

"Just barely," Seth said, teeth clenched, water dripping from his brow. He held the crown tightly.

Behind them, Zar's ship cracked. Lightning split its mast, and fire erupted from its core. The black vessel broke in two, sinking fast into the churning sea.

The battle was over.

The water calmed. The sky brightened. But in the mist, deep below, a single glowing eye opened.

Zar had lost.

As the Stormrider sailed into the horizon and the wreckage faded behind them, the mist thickened. From beneath the water, a pale hand reached up and grasped a floating piece of charred debris. Fingers curled around the wood, steady and deliberate.

But in the deep, the tide still whispered his name.

Chapter 25

The Long Voyage

The sea was quiet now, but the Stormrider bore the

scars of battle. Her sails were torn, her masts cracked, and her hull groaned with every wave. The once-proud vessel limped across the open sea, held together by grit, rope, and the will of her crew. The battle had been won, but the cost was steep—and their journey far from over.

Captain Greaves stood at the helm, jaw tight. "She won't make it quickly back to Melbonia," he said. "Not with this damage. But we'll make it—slowly, and with luck."

Melbonia. Their home port. The name stirred both hope and heaviness in the crew. It meant a return to familiar waters—but also a long, uncertain voyage ahead with a wounded ship. There would be no easy homecoming this time.

The journey took weeks. The Stormrider moved slowly, its wounded frame creaking with every swell. During the long days and colder nights, the crew worked in silence or sang old songs to pass the time. The sea stayed calm, as if exhausted from the fury it had unleashed.

Below deck, Zavalla recovered in his bunk, pale but slowly gaining strength. One night, under starlight, he joined Seth near the stern.

"You saved me," Zavalla said quietly, his eyes on the dark horizon.

Seth didn't respond right away.

"I've never had anyone fight for me," Zavalla continued. "Not like that. I was raised by wizards. Feared by most. Loyalty... it's not something I've understood. Not until now."

Seth glanced over, surprised by the vulnerability. "You'd do the same for us."

Zavalla offered a tight nod. "I think I would. And that terrifies me."

Elsewhere on the deck, Ro stood by the rails, watching the moonlight flicker on the waves. Seth joined her sometimes. They talked about the journey, about where they might go next, about nothing at all. Something unspoken grew between them with each quiet moment—a fragile closeness built not from words, but shared glances and the comfort of silence. Neither dared to name it, but it lingered in the spaces between their footsteps.

Ember, too, had changed. The weeks at sea gave her time to grow. She trained with the crew—soaring, diving, catching tossed fruit in the air. Her wings stretched wider than before, and the fire she breathed burned hotter. Milo swore she understood more than ever, responding to his commands with sharp chirps and gleaming eyes.

Milo whistled as he stirred a dented pot over a makeshift brazier near the bow.
"If this ship doesn't sink, it'll be because she's fueled by stew and stubbornness," he muttered, then offered Ember a slice of smoked fish. "For morale, not magic."

A shout rang out from the crow's nest—"Land!"
The crew rushed to the rails, silence giving way to cautious cheers. Some wept. Others just stared, not sure if the shape on the horizon was real or just something they'd been imagining in their sleep.

By the time the faint peaks of Melbonia's cliffs rose on the horizon, the Stormrider was barely floating. But within the crew, something stronger had formed—a resilience, a unity forged by storms, betrayal, and the reclaiming of a treasure thought lost to time.

And as the sun dipped low and the sails flapped in a weary wind, they steered toward home, unaware of the truths, trials, and ghosts that would soon rise in its shadow.

Chapter 26

Return to Port Melbonia

he Stormrider limped into Port Melbonia, its tattered

sails flapping in the sea breeze, barely drawing a glance from the workers and traders swarming the busy docks. Smoke from cooking fires mingled with the salt air, and wary figures eyed the vessel with both curiosity and caution.

Captain Greaves handled the harbor formalities swiftly, offering a portion of the recovered treasure hoard in exchange for repairs and docking rights. With a firm handshake and a glint of steel behind his eyes, he ensured his crew would be left alone—for now.

As a final gesture of gratitude, Greaves turned to Seth and the others.

"Take first pick," he said. "You've earned that much, and more."

Seth stepped forward, drawn by an almost magnetic pull. The Aquarian Crown, nestled among the treasure, shimmered as he reached for it. As his fingers brushed its surface, it came alive —glowing with a soft blue light. The others stared in silence. The crown had chosen him.

Off to the side, Zavalla watched, arms folded. His face was unreadable, but in his eyes—deep and shadowed—there lingered the weight of what might have been. After a long moment, he stepped forward and silently picked up an obsidian ring Its surface, dark as the void, was etched with strange runes that pulsed faintly with a silvery-blue light. An iron eagle was set into the band itself, wings spread as if in flight.. It pulsed once in his hand, like a quiet heartbeat. He slipped it onto his finger without a word, and returned to the shadows near the wall. The storm, the sinking ship, the drowning of the crown… they had averted it all. Just barely.

Ro stepped forward next, her gaze flicking past ornate blades and rings until it fell on a small leather case lined with throwing daggers. The hilts were curved and balanced perfectly for speed and stealth, each engraved with a silver hawk motif. She picked them up without hesitation.

"These'll do nicely," she said with a smirk.

Milo rummaged through a crate of oddities and shiny trinkets until he emerged holding a copper cooking pot with a dragon-shaped handle. "Oh-ho! Look at you," he cooed. "You'll make stew and history." He added a pouch of exotic spices and a steel ladle to his belt.

Ember poked her snout into a velvet-lined chest and chirped at a chunk of smooth volcanic glass. When Seth held it up, it shimmered faintly with inner heat. He offered it to her, and she curled around it, purring like a contented cat.

They remained in Port Melbonia for a few days, repairing what they could of the Stormrider. The group spent one last night aboard, joined by laughter, food, and bittersweet memories. Milo cooked an enormous farewell meal—roasted sea fowl, honeyed root vegetables, and warm berry tarts. Even Zavalla cracked a rare smile.

When the ship finally prepared to leave again, Milo stood near the gangplank, exchanging hugs and awkward goodbyes.

Tears welled in Ro's eyes. Even Zavalla cleared his throat suspiciously. Seth gave Milo a firm clasp on the shoulder.

"You be safe out there," he said.

The crew began boarding. The ship's ropes were untied. The Stormrider set sail. The group stood at the dock, waving with tears in their eyes.

Then—from behind them:

"Why is everyone crying?" came Milo's voice.

The group turned to see him standing proudly on the dock, pack slung over his shoulder, hat crooked, and grin wide.

"Should I be crying too? Or are we all just being dramatic?" he asked, then added with mock indignation, "You really think I'd let you lot run off without me? You'd starve by the second day. Get all skinny and miserable."

Ro laughed through her tears. Seth just shook his head.

"Welcome back," Zavalla muttered, half-smiling.

Together again, the group turned from the docks, the weight of the ocean behind them and the promise of new paths ahead.

Chapter 27

The Bard s Song

he Rusty Turtle, a tavern near the beach in Port

Melbonia, had once been an ancient mechanical sea turtle—
one of the rusted submarines built by the old world before
dragons reduced the cities to ash. Now repurposed into a
drinking hall, its hollow iron frame echoed with voices and the
clatter of mugs. Flickering lanterns dangled from twisted pipes
and exposed beams, casting light across the rounded chamber
that had once housed the engine core. Salt and rust mingled
with the scents of roasting fish and spiced ale. Milo was deep
in conversation with the cook about the proper ratio of kickroot
to pepperblossom in a stew.

But then, the lute rang out.

The bard on the small stage wore a patchwork green coat and
had a voice like velvet rubbed across stone. He strummed
slowly, drawing attention from every corner of the room. Seth,
Ro, Zavalla, and the others turned to listen.

"High in the Snow-Capped Mountains' crown, Where crystal
giants guard the ground, A glow of green, a cave of stone,
Where brave men came and died alone…"

He sang of the first adventurers who mistook a jagged peak for
a crystal monument. Upon reaching it, they discovered the
truth: a monstrous, glowing creature—six arms, eight wings—
standing sentinel before the cave. Fifteen fighters and wizards
fought. Two fled into the cave and found the source of the

green glow. One was torn apart. The other, a fighter named Zabris, escaped with the tale.

"She told of wings that swept the air, Of shining claws and emerald glare, A treasure pulsed inside the dark, A crystal gem with living spark."

The bard paused only for a beat, then shifted the rhythm and began the next part of the song:

"In deepest woods where no light dared, A rider came, green-armored, spared. His steed was black, its eyes aglow, Through forest dark he'd nightly go.

For every beast or demon slain, He'd kneel beside it in the rain, And chant the words no man could speak, While shadows curled and light grew weak.

He'd point his blade—so short, so bright, And green fire turned death to light. Each corpse erased, each wound undone, By rituals no soul could run.

But then on Elson's 16th final breath, A spirit came, as pale as death, With wings of white and eightfold spread, It echoed back the words he said.

The rider vanished, blade in hand, No mark was left upon the land. And some believe the saber true, Was hidden where none could pursue."

The bard's voice dropped to a whisper.

"They say the white-winged being took the saber to a place beyond reach. That no mortal hands may wield it again."

Silence fell once more before the usual noise returned to the Rusty Turtle. But at Seth's table, the group exchanged glances.

"That cave in the mountains," Zavalla murmured. "The green glow... that has to be the Gauntlets."

Ro tapped the table. "And Zabris Yansâ. She survived. I remember that name. She lives in Zarnoth."

Seth leaned forward. "Then that's where we go next."

Before anyone could reply, Milo clapped loudly. "Absolutely. But first, can we all agree that this place makes the best fish stew in Acklelend?"

The bard, overhearing, raised his mug toward them. "Good luck finding the Crystal Mountain. And beware the thing that guards it."

Zavalla nodded grimly. "We will."

Chapter 28

North to Zarnoth

he morning mist had not yet lifted from Port Melbonia when the group gathered just beyond the market square. Ships creaked in their moorings, and the cries of gulls echoed between the buildings. The events of the past few days—the bard's haunting song, the revelation of the Crystal Mountain, and the legend of the monstrous guardian—still lingered like smoke in their minds. The image of a jagged peak with a cave of glowing with green energy, and the lone survivor who had returned to tell the tale, weighed heavily on them all.

Zavalla stood quietly at the edge of the square, his cloak drawn tight despite the rising sun. The salt wind teased the edges of his hood, but he remained still, eyes fixed on the sky above the rooftops—as if watching something far beyond. His thoughts, though unspoken, seemed to swirl with the gravity of what lay ahead.

"Zabris Yansâ," he muttered. "If she survived that mountain... she may know how to guide us."

Ro adjusted her cloak and glanced toward the harbor, where crews loaded barrels and crates onto northbound wagons. She moved with purpose, but her eyes lingered on the road signs pointing north. Her jaw was tight, her shoulders slightly hunched. She hadn't been back to Zarnoth since she ran away—not since everything changed. The thought of returning now twisted in her gut like a knot of smoke. But she said nothing.

She couldn't. Not without revealing the truth she'd buried deep.

"We'll need supplies and transport," she said instead, steadying her voice. "If the bard's tale holds truth, we're walking into danger. We need to be ready."

Milo scratched at his chin and frowned. "A crystal mountain guarded by a flying beast with too many wings? Doesn't exactly sound welcoming. Think they've got a tavern up there?"

Ro snorted. "Only if you're okay with ghost stew and nightmares for dessert."

Seth nodded, his hand brushing the crown secured in his pack. The Aquarian Crown had glowed softly the night before, pulsing like a heartbeat. He glanced at Zavalla, then at Ro, his expression tightening.

"We go to Zarnoth first," he said. "To find Zabris. And then to Crystal Mountain."

Zavalla raised a brow. "You speak as if the road will unfold neatly before us. Zarnoth has its shadows, too. Don't expect a warm welcome."

"Then we won't wait for one," Ro replied. "We've faced worse."

Milo adjusted the pot on his head, tilting it like a noble's helm. "Well, I've never cooked at high altitude," he said. "But I have a feeling I'll be inventing snow soup before long."

Ro's voice softened. "You think she'll talk to us? Zabris? She lost her whole expedition. Maybe she's done with the past."

Seth shrugged. "Maybe. But she came back. That means something. And if anyone knows what we're about to face, it's her."

Ember chirped, then flapped up onto a stack of crates near the edge of the square, curling her tail around one as she perched. Her molten amber eyes flicked between the group, glowing brighter with each passing day. She had grown bolder lately, always keeping a high vantage point to watch over them—as if sensing the tension beneath their words.

As the group set off, their boots kicked up dew from the cobblestones. The air was crisp, the smell of salt slowly giving way to pine and loam as they climbed away from the coast. Birds called in the distance, and wagons rumbled past, the drivers eyeing the group with cautious curiosity.

On the second day of their journey, they encountered a curious figure camped at the base of an ancient willow tree, surrounded by small wooden carvings of animals and herbs.

"Ho there!" the man called as they approached. He wore mismatched boots, a wide-brimmed hat with feathers stuck in the band, and a patchy vest that smelled faintly of moss. "You lot look like you're going somewhere very important. Or very dangerous. Maybe both."

Milo leaned toward Ro and whispered, "He looks like a spice merchant fell into a patch of mushrooms."

"That's Calus Lom," Zavalla said quietly, his eyes narrowing with a mix of wariness and recognition. "Used to be a scholar. Now... well, people say he's a few marbles short."

Calus beamed and waved them closer. "Former author of botanical texts, yes indeed! And now proud wanderer of Acklelend's wilds. You're heading north, aren't you? Zarnoth?

151

You'll want to avoid the stone-hag trails near the forked ridge. I'd be happy to show you a safer way—if you trade me a story. Or a song. Or... perhaps a bowl of stew?"

Milo brightened. "Now we're speaking my language. Stew first, song after."

They camped with Calus for the evening, sharing tales and laughing well into the night. At one point, as the fire danced and the stars wheeled slowly overhead, Calus leaned closer to the flames and said in a wistful voice, "You know, I once danced with a dragon."

Milo raised an eyebrow. "That sounds like something I'd say after too much spiced cider."

Calus chuckled. "No, truly. I was younger then, out documenting moss growth in the Deepwood Glens for a book on forest flora. I'd been walking for days, speaking to trees— because no one else would listen—when I came upon her. A woman, cloaked in green, with eyes like summer leaves. She was humming some old tune, barefoot in the moss. I danced with her in a circle of moonlight."

Ro looked up from her cup. "What happened?"

"She smiled," Calus said, eyes twinkling. "Then froze. Backed away. And turned into a dragon—green, scaled, radiant. Before I could ask her name, she flew off into the trees, vanishing into the sky like smoke."

Zavalla gave him a sidelong look. "You're lucky she didn't eat you."

"Nonsense," Calus replied. "She liked the way I twirled."

They all laughed, unsure how much of it was truth or tale—but none of them forgot the story. As the fire crackled and stars pricked the canopy above, Milo volunteered to make stew—his usual gesture of hospitality. Using the copper pot he'd taken from the treasure hoard on the lost island, he filled it with herbs, root vegetables, and dried meat.

The group didn't think much of it at first, but as the stew began to simmer, Calus leaned closer and blinked.

"That's no ordinary pot," he muttered. "I've seen plenty of cookware in my wandering years, but that... that's humming."

Milo tilted his head. "What do you mean, humming?"

Calus pointed. "Listen."

Sure enough, as the bubbling continued, the pot emitted a faint hum—low and melodic, like a lullaby from a dream.

"It's warming evenly, too," Milo added, surprised. "Even the best copper shouldn't hold this kind of heat without scorching."

"It's responding to you," Calus said with growing curiosity. "There's magic in that metal. Might be old... very old. Careful what you cook in it. It might remember."

That night, the stew came out richer and more flavorful than any meal they'd had in weeks. It was warm in a way that lingered—not just in the belly, but in the heart. Even Zavalla seemed at ease, and Ember fell asleep curled against Milo with a full belly and a rare purr.

The group went to sleep by the firelight, the pot cooling silently beside them, its surface no longer glowing—but not entirely still either. Though odd, Calus proved helpful, drawing a map with shortcuts only a true wanderer would know. He spoke of spirits in the high woods and warned them of rumors that something had awakened near the northern trails— something old. When they parted ways the next morning, he gave them a carved wooden figurine of a pine squirrel.

"To guide you in dark woods," he said. "Or at least to make you laugh."

The road carried them past windswept farmland and abandoned outposts swallowed by creeping vines. Each town they passed grew smaller, quieter, as they neared the wilder parts of the northern lands. Local travelers warned them of strange weather and bandit sightings near the foothills, but none of it swayed them. Zarnoth was calling.

The days grew colder as they pressed northward. Milo kept their spirits lifted with songs and terrible puns. Ro scouted ahead, sometimes disappearing for hours before reappearing like a shadow with a warning or a smirk. Zavalla often walked alone, murmuring to himself or scribbling into his worn spellbook. Seth watched them all—quiet, thoughtful, uncertain.

One night, as they sat around a crackling fire beneath a sky smeared with stars, Seth finally spoke.

"Do you think we're ready for what's coming?"

Ro didn't answer right away. She poked the fire with a stick, the flames flaring. "I think we're as ready as we'll ever be. And that scares me."

Zavalla didn't look up. "You'll never be ready. That's not the point. The point is going anyway."

"Well," Milo said, stirring a pot of stew, "as long as we go with full bellies, I think we'll be fine."

154

As the savory scent wafted from the bubbling pot, Milo furrowed his brow and lifted the lid with a ladle in hand. The copper gleamed unnaturally in the firelight. "Huh," he muttered. "That's strange... this pot's holding heat like it's enchanted or something."

Ro leaned in with narrowed eyes. "Is that smoke... changing color?"

Indeed, thin wisps of steam curled upward in shimmering hues—golden, then green, then pale silver. Milo chuckled, clearly delighted. "Well, that's new. Maybe this isn't just any pot. Maybe it's a magic stew enhancer. Or maybe it likes me."

"Or maybe it's cursed," Zavalla said dryly, though he didn't seem alarmed—only intrigued.

Ember sniffed the pot and chirped approvingly, curling beside Milo's feet.

"We'll keep an eye on it," Seth said with a half-smile. "But if it starts talking or growing legs, we're leaving it behind."

"Deal," Milo said cheerfully. "But not until after dessert."

They all laughed—softly, warily. The wind shifted again, and the faintest outline of Zarnoth's spires appeared in the distance, glimmering beneath the pale morning light.

What they would find there—and what waited in the cold heart of the mountain—none of them could yet imagine.

Chapter 29

The Stranger Returns

everal days after leaving Port Melbonia, the group made camp beneath a crooked cedar tree at the edge of a wind-swept meadow. Nearby, a patch of Coupra plants grew in the soft earth—brown, leafy spheres resting on the ground with long, sprouting leaves rising from their tops. Milo had warned the others not to get too close to the bulbous bases, which housed poisonous liquid prized by alchemists. Ro had mentioned once that Scoofins liked to burrow into them like tiny, grumpy squatters. The stars glimmered between passing clouds, and the faint sounds of frogs echoed from a shallow stream nearby. Milo stirred a pot of stew over the fire, humming a song that made no sense and chuckling to himself whenever Ember nudged him with her nose.

Ro sat sharpening her daggers, her eyes darting now and then toward the darkness beyond the firelight. Seth leaned against a boulder, his fingers brushing the crown hidden in his pack. Zavalla sat nearby, cross-legged, sketching arcane circles into his worn leather-bound book. Tension still clung to their silence, unspoken worries humming just below the surface.

Then the fire froze.

The wind stopped. The frogs fell silent. Even Ember, mid-nudge, halted as if suspended in glass. Only the soft crackle of magic remained.

From the edge of the meadow, a familiar presence stepped forward.

The air shimmered. A cloaked figure emerged from the shadows—his form more defined than ever before. His tattered white-blue cloak drifted in a breeze that no longer moved. Hornlike ridges arced subtly beneath the cowl, and faint scales glimmered across his exposed hands. His presence carried weight, as though time itself bowed around him. The group rose slowly, unsure whether to speak or reach for weapons.

The stranger's voice echoed, layered and low, like multiple tones resonating at once.

"You've changed the current."

Seth stepped forward, hand near his sword. "What do you mean?"

"In my time, the Aquarian Crown was lost—claimed by the sea, never to be seen again. Because of you, it survives. Because of you, Zarnoth still stands."

A long pause followed. Even the fire, though still frozen, seemed to pulse with invisible breath, as though time held its own exhale.

Ro narrowed her eyes. "Why are you helping us? Who are you really?"

The figure remained silent. He turned his gaze toward the distant trees, as if searching memories that hadn't yet happened.

"There is a force that twists what should be. It wears the guise of fate and uses the stones of time to bend the river. I have seen what follows. The mountain will awaken. The crown has chosen. The storm was only the beginning."

Zavalla took a step closer, eyes narrowed. "You speak like you know us. But you hide your face."

The stranger's voice faltered—just for a heartbeat. "Because I must. For now."

He turned to Seth, and the energy between them seemed to shift.

"The mountain holds more than stone. When you stand before it, remember who you are—not what you were told."

Then time released.

The fire snapped. Wind surged. Ember blinked and snorted in confusion. Milo dropped his ladle with a loud metallic thunk.

"Ok what'd I miss? Who was that?" he asked.

Seth stood still, fists clenched. Ro's eyes searched his face, then turned to Zavalla, who remained silent. His jaw was tight. His eyes—far away.

Later, when they asked him again, Zavalla said only, "Whoever that was… he's walking a line we may all cross one day."

But when Zavalla thought no one watched, he sat longer than usual beside the embers. His eyes tracked the shadows, and his fingers hovered over his dragon-marked arm.

Chapter 30

The Walls of Zarnoth

he morning ride toward Zarnoth was tense, their path winding through thickets of tall grass and sparse groves of willow and redbrush trees. The stranger's visit the night before had left more than unease—it had cracked something open between them.

"We still don't know who he is," Ro said, her voice low but sharp. "He could be trying to help, or trying to steer us. We know what the Time Stone can do."

Zavalla trailed behind the group, seated upon a softly glowing, summoned creature—part stag, part shadow, with curling antlers and hooved feet that barely touched the ground. It shimmered faintly with arcane light as it carried him, sparing his damaged legs the strain of travel. Seth cast a glance his way.

"We've also met you," Seth said quietly. "You've helped us. We wouldn't be here without you."

"Which is exactly why it's complicated," Ro replied. "What if he's the one rewriting things?"

Milo, walking beside Ember, scratched his chin. "Okay, but can someone tell me—who exactly is this guy? Last night was the first time I saw him. You're all talking like this is normal."

Ro glanced over her shoulder. "He showed up once before. Froze time. Told us to find Zavalla. Disappeared."

"And you didn't think to mention that before the creepy glowing guy came back?" Milo asked, wide-eyed.

"We were a bit busy with sinking temples and sea battles," Seth muttered.

Milo huffed. "Fair. Still… he didn't attack us. Gave us a warning, if anything. I say that puts him one ladle ahead of most villains."

"Or he's playing a long game," Ro muttered.

Zavalla finally spoke. "Whoever he is, he's further down this path than any of us. That means he's either trying to fix a mistake… or ensure it happens."

Their conversation faded into silence as the city came into view, rising like a memory from Ro's past. Their thoughts stayed fixed on the flickering silhouette and the riddle he had become.

Zarnoth's towers clawed at the morning sky, their tips catching the sun's first light in gleaming hues of silver and red. High walls ringed the city—imposing and ancient—lined with watchful guards in polished scale armor. The city gates loomed wide but heavily patrolled, their iron portcullis raised just high enough for caravans to pass beneath.

The group stood on the crest of a hill overlooking the outer district. Smoke from a dozen hearths drifted lazily above stone rooftops, and bells rang faintly in the distance.

Ro pulled her cloak tighter around her face. Her jaw was tense, eyes shaded by the hood. She hadn't spoken much that morning.

"We don't have to go through the main gate," Seth offered.

Ro shook her head. "We do. It's faster. And safer than sneaking around the wall. But once we're in… let me handle the talking."

Seth exchanged a glance with Milo, who simply shrugged and tightened his belt.

Zavalla's eyes swept the skyline, lingering on the tallest tower —the Spire of Records. "If Zabris is still alive, that's where her identity will be buried. The Council of Guilds keeps all migration and survivor records locked away inside."

They approached the city slowly, blending with a merchant caravan and a line of tradesmen. Guards asked few questions— thanks in part to a bribe from Milo, who slipped a handful of rare spices into a nervous officer's palm.

Inside the gates, the city buzzed. Stone bridges spanned canals that split the city into levels. Banners of house emblems fluttered from balconies. Bells tolled on the hour, joined by the voices of hawkers selling everything from fried rootfruit to enchanted hair tonics.

Ro led them quickly through the winding streets. She moved like someone who had memorized every alley, every shortcut —but avoided eye contact with every patrol.

They found a modest inn tucked near a statue of a forgotten knight. Milo insisted on ordering a full meal for the group before they made any plans.

Later, with bellies full and cloaks drying by the hearth, Ro spread a folded map on the table.

"She's kept a low profile for years, no official records or public appearances. I know someone who might help us find her—Imah Vury Gude, master of the Zarnoth Swordsman Guild. He trains fighters, adventurers, sellswords... and he keeps tabs on everyone who comes through his doors. If she's hiding in plain sight, he'll know. And he owes me a favor. A big one."

Zavalla raised a brow. "You trust him?"

Ro looked away. "Let's just say Vury much," she said with a sly grin and a wink.

Seth leaned in. "Then that's where we start."

From the shadowed corner of the inn, unseen, a pair of eyes watched them over a mug of bitter ale. The man's gaze lingered longer than most. He wore a travel-stained cloak and a ring with a hawk crest. He had the look of someone who recognized opportunity—and how to twist it.

Jackom Halfdill smiled without warmth.

"Well now," he whispered. "Ain't this getting interesting."

Chapter 31

Swords of the Past

he next morning, the streets of Zarnoth buzzed with
the clamor of carts and voices, but the group moved quietly. Ro
led them across a narrow bridge strung with ivy, her cloak
pulled tight and hood low. Seth, Milo, Zavalla, and Ember
followed, keeping pace as they crossed into a quieter district of
the city where stone paths curved between old buildings and
watchful eyes. Pigeons scattered from low windowsills, and the
scent of baked bread mingled with the sharper tang of forge
smoke drifting from somewhere nearby.

The Zarnoth Swordsman Guild sat at the edge of a market
square, its bright banners hanging proudly above the carved
archway. Inside, the clang of blades and barked commands
echoed through the halls. They passed students in practice
duels, sweat flying as wooden swords clashed. Some paused to
stare at the newcomers—especially at Ember—but most
returned to their drills.

Imah Vury Gude stood near the back of the hall, his arms
crossed, watching a sparring match with one critical eye and
one half-smile. He was older than Ro remembered, his beard
streaked with silver and a long scar curling across his left
cheek. He turned as they approached, eyes widening slightly.

"Well, well," he said, lowering his arms slowly, his eyes
widening as he took in the cloaked figure before him. For a

163

moment, he said nothing, the recognition hitting like a sword to the gut. "Ro?" he whispered.

Ro gave him a subtle shake of the head, her eyes locking with his in silent warning. Not here. Not now. She gave a faint nod toward a side door near the training hall—a quiet room used for private instruction, one they both knew well.

Imah's mouth closed, jaw tightening as he straightened. His gaze flicked to Seth and Zavalla, measuring their presence with a subtle wariness, as if trying to read how much they already knew. Without a word, he turned and led them toward the indicated room, waving off a student who stared. "Get back to your training!" he barked before leaving the main hall. His voice, when it returned, was smoother, practiced. "If it isn't Ro of a Hundred Names. And here I thought you'd been hanged or crowned by now."

"Not yet," Ro replied. "But it's been close."

He took a step closer, lowering his voice with a hint of old frustration beneath the jest. "Your father is furious, you know. I told you to take control of your life—not vanish into the wilds and play fugitive. He didn't expect this. Neither did I."

Ro shot him a sharp look—another silent warning with the others still present. Her expression hardened.

"Who cares how he feels?" she muttered. "You've done more for me than he ever has. You raised me with a sword in one hand and a lesson in the other. You were the one who actually saw me."

His eyes lingered on her, and for the briefest flicker, concern softened his expression. He had trained her since she could hold a blade. Her disappearance had shaken him more than he'd ever admitted. A thousand questions lay unsaid behind his eyes, but he respected the wall she'd thrown up.

Imah's gaze drifted to the others. "You've brought friends. And a dragon. I'd ask for introductions, but I'm guessing this isn't a social call."

"No," Ro said. "We're looking for someone. A woman named Zabris Yansâ. A Gromin. She was part of the Crystal Mountain expedition. She survived. We heard she's here."

Imah didn't react right away. He studied Ro, then glanced toward Zavalla, whose expression had turned cold and unreadable. Ember shifted her wings near the door, watching him intently.

"I know the name," he said at last. "And the story. Fifteen dead, one survivor. Zabris doesn't talk about it. Not to anyone. But she's alive. And yes—she's still in the city."

Ro's voice softened. "Can you tell us where to find her?"

Imah's smile faded. "You sure you want to?"

Seth stepped forward. "We don't have a choice. The path we're on leads through that mountain. And if there's even a chance she can help us survive it, we need to speak with her."

Imah studied them all for a long moment, then finally nodded. "There's a boarding house just off the Ironstairs. Quiet place. She keeps to herself. You didn't hear it from me."

"Thank you," Ro said.

Before they left, he reached out briefly, laying a hand on Ro's shoulder. "I meant what I said all those years ago. You were always stronger than they let you believe."

165

Ro looked at him, and for a moment, something softened in her gaze. Then she turned and led the others into the street, toward the next step of their journey.

He looked at her one last time. "Stay safe my child and return home again... someday."

Chapter 32

The Last Survivor

The boarding house off the Ironstairs looked like any

other in the quieter districts of Zarnoth—plain shutters, a crooked chimney, and ivy creeping up weathered stone walls. But to Ro, it stood out. It was too quiet. The kind of quiet that held history.

Zavalla knocked.

After a long pause, the door creaked open a few inches. A weathered Gromin woman peered out. Her features bore the telltale marks of her people—tanned, leathery skin patterned with faded black stripes, and eyes like polished obsidian. Her hair, streaked with white, was pulled back into a tight braid. One hand, strong despite its age, rested on the doorframe as if expecting to need it for balance—or defense. Her eyes were sharp and cautious.

"Yes?"

"Zabris Yansâ?" Seth asked.

The woman didn't answer right away. Her gaze lingered on each of them—especially Zavalla—then slowly opened the door wider.

"Come inside."

167

The interior was modest but clean. Shelves lined with books and scrolls covered one wall, and a kettle hissed gently above a low hearth. Zabris moved with the weight of someone who had survived too many things.

"I know why you're here," she said before they could ask. "Same thing everyone wants from me. You want to know about the mountain."

Seth nodded. "We need to get inside. And survive it."

Zabris sat, motioned for them to do the same. "Most don't. And those who try either don't come back or wish they hadn't."

She hesitated at first, her voice catching in her throat. The memories weighed heavily on her, as if speaking them aloud might make them real again.

"We climbed with hope," she said. "But the mountain had other plans. The air turned cold as we approached the summit. Then it appeared—the guardian. Towering. Six arms. Eight wings. Veins of emerald light across skin harder than stone. It didn't speak. Just... moved. Like it had been waiting."

She paused, eyes flicking to the fire. "I fought. We all did. I tried to hold the line while the others cast spells. We used everything we had. Nothing worked."

Zabris's hands tightened. "But then one of the alchemists— Rellen—used a flask of Rockworm acid. It burned the creature's leg. Slowed it. For the first time, it reacted—like it felt pain.

"We fought. We died," she said. "It tore through our mages first. Shattered our barrier spells like they were paper. Some ran. Another and I made it into the mountain. One didn't make it out."

"What did you see inside?" Ro asked.

Zabris looked into the fire. "There was a chamber. Carved smooth, glowing. At its heart was a figure—encased in crystal. A man in green armor, perfectly preserved. Like a statue... or a prisoner."

Zavalla leaned forward. "Was he alive?"

"I think so. The air changed when we got close. The light pulsed. And I saw them—Gauntlets, wrapped in vines etched with emerald light. Worn on his hands, fused into the armor itself. They pulsed when we drew near, like they recognized us. I'm certain it was the Gauntlets of Verdance. But the guardian came crashing in, and I ran. It killed the last of my companions before I could reach him."

Her voice faltered, and for a heartbeat, she looked older—like the memory itself was carved into her. She took a long breath and continued. "But the guardian came crashing in, and I ran. It killed the last of my companions before I could reach him."

A silence fell.

"You'll need more than courage. You'll need crystal vials. Rockworm acid. And a reason stronger than survival. Otherwise, the mountain will break you."

She fixed them each with a level gaze. "You'll need to follow the pass through Devil's Falls. From there, make your way into the Nowin Kingdom. Speak with King Frizgorn. He controls access to the mountain's sacred perimeter. He won't be quick to trust—but if you tell him Zabris Yansâ sent you, he'll listen."

Outside, the wind howled down the Ironstairs. But inside, a path had truly begun to take shape.

Chapter 33

Through Devil's Falls

he journey eastward from Zarnoth took several days,
winding through stretches of wild countryside and broken
roads. They passed south of the ruins of Loopkin—its shattered
towers and scorched stone now silent monuments to the past.
To the south, through breaks in the forest canopy, they
glimpsed the dark, mist-wreathed lake that cradled the Isle of
the Dead. The path bent and twisted, more a memory of a road
than anything maintained.

They traveled cautiously. The weight of what they'd learned
from Zabris clung to them like mist. Ro kept to the lead,
cloaked and quiet, her eyes constantly scanning the brush. Milo
made light of the trek at first, but even his humor grew thin as
the terrain worsened. Seth and Zavalla kept the middle, the
latter riding his summoned spectral stag, its silent hooves
gliding over mud and stone without sound.

During their quiet moments—while setting up camp or walking
side by side along long forest stretches—Seth and Ro began to
open up to each other in ways they hadn't before.

"You aren't always this quiet on the road." Seth said one
evening, poking at the fire with a stick.

Ro, sitting across from him, smirked. "Only when I'm thinking. Or trying not to think."

"What are you trying not to think about?" he asked, watching the firelight flicker in her eyes.

She shrugged but didn't look away. "Home. The people I left behind. Things I can't fix."

He nodded slowly. "I get that. I still see my father's face sometimes. It never really goes away."

For a moment, the silence between them felt fuller. Not heavy, but shared.

Ro broke it gently. "You know, you're easier to talk to out here."

Seth smiled, a little surprised. "Must be the trees. They don't interrupt."

That made her laugh—genuinely. "And here I thought you were all shield and brooding silences."

Seth chuckled softly. "Guilty. But I make exceptions for clever rogues with sharp tongues."

Later, as the group settled into sleep, Ro lingered at the edge of the firelight beside him. She didn't say anything, just sat close, her shoulder nearly brushing his.

They didn't speak of it directly. But the bond between them had shifted. What had once been wary respect had become something deeper. Something real.

After days of travel, the land began to change. Cliffs rose around them, twisting red formations like jagged spears erupting from the earth. The air thickened with the scent of sulfur and mineral-rich steam. The sound of crashing water echoed from farther ahead—constant and powerful.

At last, Devil's Falls loomed into view.

It looked like a broken stairway carved by giants—twisting stone bridges that arched over venomous waters and cascades so powerful they shuddered the cliffs around them. Mist clung low to the gorge, hiding sudden drops and narrow ledges. The group paused at the edge of the cliff, staring in quiet awe.

They moved cautiously along the winding path, each step echoing across the canyon walls. Ember padded ahead, wings tight to her body. Seth kept a hand on his shield, while Ro continued to lead, her expression unreadable. Milo walked at the rear, turning now and then to check for followers. The roar of the falls was deafening.

They weren't alone.

Back in Zarnoth, Jackom Halfdill had quietly taken notice. He had recognized Ro. Not as a thief. Not as an adventurer. But as something else, a very large bounty on her head.

That recognition alone had nearly made him act. Nearly. But then he'd overheard them speaking—whispers of a journey east to the Nowin Kingdom, through Devil's Falls, and something hidden in the Crystal Mountain. Treasure. Rare. Magical. Valuable enough that they were willing to risk their lives for it.

So Jackom made a decision.

Why settle for just the bounty, when he could have the treasure too?

He followed them from the inn, slipping through alley shadows and market crowds, always careful, always watching. Now, he trailed them far enough behind to avoid suspicion, but close enough to learn where they camped. If they survived the journey... he'd be waiting. Let them do the hard work. He'd swoop in at the end and take it all.

Both the gold and the girl.

And no one would see him coming.

The stone beneath their boots slicked with moisture, and the air buzzed with strange life.

"I hate this place," Milo muttered. "It smells like something died and then boiled itself."

"It's not the smell you should worry about," Zavalla warned. "This place breathes danger."

Just ahead, a blur of motion zipped across the path—a small, round creature rolling frantically from one rock to another. Its jelly-like, bluish-purple body shimmered faintly in the light.

"Was that... a jellyball?" Milo whispered.

"Orbals," Zavalla said. " They live here. Scared of everything."

"And they should be," Zavalla added darkly. "This place is crawling with Razor Bats. Nasty things. Winged teeth, hunger for Orbals. And if we see one, more won't be far behind."

Another Orbal rolled into view, paused, and blinked up at them with wide, glassy eyes before it squeaked and vanished behind a stone column.

173

"Most mine orbs deep in the Troll Caverns," Zavalla said, recalling something he'd read. "The trolls use them. Enslave them. These ones must've escaped."

"They're harmless," Zavalla added. "But if one explodes, it'll spawn more of itself. Keep your distance, or you'll end up in a jelly stampede."

The group pressed on, navigating spiraling walkways that narrowed to mere ledges. At one point, the only way forward was a curved bridge spanning a sheer drop—rushing water foamed beneath them, crashing onto a bed of spiked stone teeth.

Suddenly, the sky above darkened. A shriek tore through the mist.

"Bats!" Milo shouted, drawing his ladle.

Out of the cliffs came winged shapes—grotesque things with leathery wings and simian bodies, jaws lined with curved fangs. The Razor Bats dove fast, shrieking for blood.

Seth raised his shield just in time to deflect one of the creatures. Ember leapt into the air, breathing a jet of fire that scorched the sky. Ro hurled one of her new throwing daggers —the silver-hilted ones she'd taken from the treasure hoard on the lost island. It shimmered strangely mid-flight, leaving a brief trail of light behind it. The dagger struck a Razor Bat cleanly between the eyes, and as it hit, there was a sudden burst of force, a small concussive pulse that knocked another nearby bat off balance. The creature tumbled and vanished into the mists below.

Before Ro could even register what had happened, the dagger reappeared in its sheath with a faint flicker of silver light, cool and whole as if it had never left.

Ro stared for a heartbeat, then drew it again, her eyes wide. "They're enchanted," she muttered. "They come back. No wonder they felt so perfectly balanced."

The fight was chaotic—slippery footing, shrieking predators, and nowhere to run.

Zavalla cast a warding pulse that shoved three Razor Bats back into the cliffs. "Keep moving!" he shouted. "We can't fight them all here!"

They ran.

Twisting paths, leaps over broken stone, slashes of wings all around them. But together, they pushed forward. The Razor Bats couldn't follow far—the terrain became too narrow for their wingspan.

At last, the group stumbled into a cavern hollowed into the cliffside, panting and bruised.

Seth pressed a hand to his ribs. "Well… that was welcoming."

Ro chuckled breathlessly. "And we're not even to the Nowin Kingdom yet."

Behind them, in the high shadows of the rock, Jackom Halfdill crouched silently. He watched the battle. He watched them survive.

He smiled.

"Just keep showing me the way," he whispered. "I'll take it from here."

Chapter 34

The Nowin Kingdom

he next morning brought pale sun filtering through mist-slick cliffs. The group broke camp quietly, the echo of Razor Bats still fresh in their minds. Wounds had been dressed. Tensions had eased slightly. But the journey wasn't over.

From the heights of Devil's Falls, they descended gradually into a low, wind-carved valley. The landscape shifted from jagged redstone to frost-laced plains scattered with ancient statues—towering figures of Nowin warriors. Their stoic postures and battle-worn forms marked the border of a realm few outsiders had ever crossed.

Feared and respected, the Nowins were formidable defenders of their icy homeland.

"That one still has a face," Milo muttered, peering into the icy stare of a Nowin knight statue missing the top of its helmet. "Creepy."

"They say this pass was once guarded by Nowin sentinels," Ro said. "This used to be part of their border."

By midday, they reached the edge of Nowin territory. "It's beautiful," Seth said softly, the weight of their journey momentarily lifted by the strange, icy serenity.

There, the path narrowed between rising hills, and from the mist emerged a towering Nowin warrior astride a monstrous Fur Dragon—an enormous beast that looked like a fusion of a Lomek and a polar bear, covered in thick white fur with gleaming horns, its wings curled against its powerful frame. Its amber eyes watched them with unsettling intelligence.

Flanking him were other Nowin guards, each mounted on a massive mountain goat ram with horns curling like iron blades. The guards wore gleaming crystal and jeweled armor etched with intricate gemwork, accented by the thick brown furs of Modoes they had slain. Their skin bore a bluish hue, and their muscular arms and legs were covered in shaggy white hair. Most striking were the two long tusks that curved downward from their upper jaw like the fangs of a sabertooth cat—a feature that made them both intimidating and uniquely Nowin. Known for their skill in crystal forging and a deadly Freeze Spell, the Nowins were a noble yet fierce race. Though their society was feudal, they were known to raid settlements and defend their mountain homeland with ruthless precision. They were also mortal enemies of the Modoes, who valued their tusks as rare trophies.

The rams stomped the earth and snorted, ready for a command.

The sight alone stopped the group in their tracks. A narrow stone gate stood crooked between two hillocks, icicles hanging from the stonework. Beyond it, the path widened into a cobbled road that curved between ancient trees, their canopies glazed with shimmering frost.

"Halt," one called. "You tread on Nowin land. State your names and business."

Ro stepped forward and bowed slightly. "We seek audience with King Frizgorn. On the word of Zabris Yansâ of Zarnoth."

The lead rider studied her, then the others. His eyes paused on Ember, on Zavalla's summoned mount, and the aquamarine glow peeking from Seth's pack.

"Follow," he said at last. "But know this—we guard our borders well. Tread carefully."

They were led through miles of winding woodland, deeper into Nowin lands. The realm revealed itself slowly: a cold, pristine expanse of tall pines and towering fur trees, their branches heavy with snow. Ice clung to every rock and root. Mountains loomed on the horizon, and the wind howled constantly through the frozen canyons. Hot springs hissed quietly near the road, casting steam into the chilled air.

Forest villages rose like sculptures of ice and timber, woven mountain side terraces glistening with frost. Irrigation channels were powered by hot spring watermills. Quiet fields of luminous grain pulsed faintly blue beneath the snowdrifts, cultivated by hardy Nowins wrapped in crystal-inset furs.

The group huddled into their cloaks. Even Ember tucked her wings tighter. Their breath fogged with each word, and by the time they reached the first village, Milo's teeth were chattering.

"We're going to need cold-weather gear," Ro muttered.

"Let's hope the king is generous," Seth replied, rubbing his hands together.

By evening, they arrived at the heart of the Nowin Kingdom— a stone fortress nestled within the high trees, its walls wrapped ice ivy and snow. Crystals set into the battlements hummed faintly with protective enchantments.

King Frizgorn awaited them beneath a canopy of crystal glass and timber, seated on a throne carved from amethyst. His eyes were pale and glacial, reflecting the icy expanse outside, and he wore no crown—only a leather circlet and a tunic of finely woven green.

When Seth gave his name, the king's expression shifted slightly.

"Bergan?" Frizgorn asked, sitting up straighter. "Romos Bergan?"

Seth blinked. "He was my father."

Frizgorn's eyes narrowed with thought. "I fought beside Romos against the Modoes, years ago. He was brave—relentless. A shame he was captured."

"Captured?" Seth echoed. "No… I was told he was killed. When I was nine."

The king regarded him carefully, his expression unreadable. "Then perhaps you were told only part of the truth."

He studied them all again, lingering on Seth and Ro, and finally Zavalla.

"I see old wounds and older blood," the king murmured. "You walk a perilous path. But perhaps it's one worth walking." nodded once. "Rest here tonight and feast! Then you'll have your answer."

179

Chapter 35

A King's Feast

he halls of King Frizgorn's fortress shimmered with golden firelight and frosted crystal. Warmth radiated from glowing stones embedded in the vaulted ceilings, battling the bite of the mountain air that crept through even the thickest stone. The grand dining hall was a marvel of craft and magic—walls sculpted from translucent ice reinforced with veins of silver, pillars carved from deep purple amethyst, and stained-glass windows that caught the waning sunlight and cast kaleidoscopic patterns across the polished stone floor. The room pulsed with quiet music, and the smell of roasted meats, spiced roots, and fresh-baked nut bread lingered like a warm blanket.

Long tables ran the length of the hall, decked in green and silver cloth. Trays of steaming food were constantly replenished by quiet Nowin attendants who moved with the grace of snowfall. Their jewel-studded armor glimmered with soft enchantments, and their expressions remained politely unreadable.

Seth sat at the edge of the table, his plate barely touched. A golden crusted roll lay untouched beside braised venison and wild onion glaze. He twirled his fork idly, eyes distant. The firelight glinted off the edge of his shield, propped behind his chair.

His father might be alive.

The thought circled endlessly in his mind, a storm that refused to settle.

Across from him, Milo was already on his second helping of flame-seared elk ribs, humming cheerfully as he devoured a spiced yam fritter.

"You know," Milo said between bites, licking sauce from his fingers, "this isn't ghost stew at all. I think I'm going to cry. If I ever disappear, tell the world I died happy, face down in Nowin gravy."

Ro chuckled softly, though her gaze lingered on Seth. She leaned toward him, her voice low enough to be carried only to him.

"You okay?"

He didn't respond immediately. The sound of silverware and distant lute music filled the silence between them.

Finally, he said, "They told me he died when I was nine. Fighting off a Modo raid near Golden Arrow. I believed it my whole life."

Ro nodded gently. "And now Frizgorn says he might be alive."

Seth's jaw tightened. "Somewhere. In chains."

Before either of them could say more, King Frizgorn rose from his high-backed chair at the head of the table. He raised a silver goblet filled with deep red wine, and his voice, though calm, carried easily through the vaulted hall.

"Tonight, you feast as honored guests. But your journey is far from over."

181

The room fell silent. Even the minstrels at the far end stilled their strings and lowered their instruments.

"You seek the peak of Crystal Mountain," Frizgorn continued. "And I would grant you safe passage—but honor must be met with honor. Romos Bergan, father of one among you, once fought beside my people during the Siege of Icebridge. He was brave, tireless, and loyal. He was captured—not slain—and if he still lives, it is in chains at a Modo prison in the fortress of the Iron Eagle near our contested northern border."

Seth slowly sat up straighter, hands clenched in his lap.

Frizgorn's gaze settled on him. "If you wish to climb the sacred slopes, you must first prove yourselves. Find Romos Bergan. Free him—or return with proof that he no longer lives. Do this, and I shall open the mountain's path to you."

Milo leaned over to Ro and muttered, "So, no dessert until we break into a Modo prison? Harsh kingdom."

Ro gave him a look, but didn't argue.

That night, after the feast had ended and the warmth of the fire faded behind him, Seth lay awake in the high guest quarters of the fortress. The room was beautiful—walls carved with stories of the Nowin people, enchanted to shimmer with gentle starlight. Crystals embedded in the stone glowed with a soft blue warmth, chasing away the chill.

But Seth couldn't sleep.

His thoughts returned again and again to the same image: a cold, dark cell. Shackles. Hollow eyes. The man he barely remembered—a voice, a laugh, a strong arm lifting him onto his shoulders as a child. Was any of that real? Or was it the dream of someone long dead?

In his restless dreams, he saw Romos again—older, worn, but alive. A whisper floated through the dark:

"Seth..."

He jolted awake, sweat slick on his brow despite the cold air. The wind howled just beyond the shutters, carrying snow and silence.

Seth stood and crossed to the narrow window. He pushed it open and let the icy air strike his face.

The mountains loomed like silent giants in the north.

Beyond them, the Modo stronghold.

Beyond that, perhaps, his father.

And beneath it all... the truth.

Chapter 36

The Iron Eagle

he sun had not yet risen when the group departed

Frizgorn's stronghold, bundled tightly in thick winter cloaks and crystal-insulated boots gifted to them by the king. Each set was crafted from Modo furs and embedded with subtle enchantments to retain warmth, a Nowin tradition passed down through mountain warlines, their breath pluming in the frostbitten air. Snowflakes drifted lazily from the sky, dusting the Nowin cobblestones in pale glitter. Seth, still shaken from the dream of his father, walked in silence near the front of the group. The others gave him space.

Ro pulled her cloak tighter as they passed through the outer gates. "You don't have to say it," she said gently, falling into step beside him. "I know this is hard."

"I need to know," Seth replied, eyes forward. "Even if he's gone, I need to see it for myself."

Behind them, Milo huffed as he tried to tighten his scarf against the biting cold. "Remind me again why the Modo can't build their prisons somewhere tropical? Maybe an island?"

"Because the cold helps break people faster," Zavalla said from atop his summoned mount. The ghostly stag glided over the icy road as if weightless. "And the Iron Eagle is more than a prison. It's a message."

The journey northward took several days, winding through valleys and across frozen rivers. The landscape changed gradually—trees thinned into jagged cliffs, and the snow lessened, hardened into icy crusts beneath their boots. Even Ember's light steps began to echo on the frozen ground. The young dragon's wings tucked tightly to her sides, smoke curling from her nostrils to warm her face.

By midday, the ruins of an old Nowin outpost emerged through the fog. Crystal shards jutted from the half-buried watchtower like broken teeth. They paused to rest.

As Milo unpacked lunch, he glanced over at Ember, who stood on a snow-covered rock nearby, wings flared slightly for balance. "You know," he said, nudging Ro, "she's grown a lot these past few weeks. Almost big enough to ride, I'd wager."

Ro raised an eyebrow. "Think she'll let you?"

Milo smirked. "One day, maybe. I mean, who wouldn't want a traveling chef with an enchanted pot riding on their back?"

He stirred a portion of stew in his copper pot, heating it over a fireless flame. The magical pot hummed quietly as the contents warmed. "Still not over how this thing works," he said. "I've cooked with every tool in Acklelend and nothing makes stew this fast. Or this good."

Ro gave him a half-smile, then turned her gaze northward. "What do we really know about the Iron Eagle?"

Zavalla shook his head. "Very little. Only that it used to be a Nowin stronghold, long ago—before the Modo took it by force. The name's all we have. No maps. No weak points. Just stories."

185

"Sounds promising," Milo muttered. "Why call it the Iron Eagle, though?"

"Some say the fortress is shaped like a great eagle carved into the cliff," Ro replied. "But that's probably just legend."

"Either way," Zavalla said, "it won't be easy getting in."

Ro raised an eyebrow. "Unwise sounds like our specialty."

As they packed up and moved on, the wind picked up, moaning through narrow canyons. A feeling of being watched crept over them.

Somewhere, unseen in the white haze, something moved.

Jackom Halfdill crouched behind a ridge of snow-dusted rock. His cloak was patched and dirty, but his grin was razor sharp. He'd followed them from the Nowin gates, careful never to be seen.

"Just keep walking," he muttered to himself. "Find the treasure. I'll find my payday."

He adjusted the gleaming dagger at his belt—one of many he had earned through deception and betrayal. But none had promised rewards like this.

At dusk, the group reached the edge of a steep ridgeline. Below, nestled between two frozen peaks, loomed a vast cliff face with a hollow carved into its heart. Within that hollow perched a massive structure wrought entirely of blackened iron —an enormous eagle with wings folded at its sides. Its eyes glowed faintly red through the snow, and steel feathers jutted outward, weathered by time but still razor-sharp. The Iron Eagle stood not as part of the mountain, but as a relic from another age, towering above what had once been a Nowin fortress, now claimed by the Modo.

Smoke rose in lazy spirals from vents near its base. Guard towers dotted the ledges, and heavy gates sealed off the narrow causeway leading to the mouth.

Ro lowered her spyglass. "There it is. The Iron Eagle."

Seth's hands clenched at his sides.

Milo whistled. "That's not a prison. That's a fortress."

Zavalla nodded. "And tonight, we find a way inside."

As the sun vanished behind the peaks, the snow fell harder, and the mountain swallowed the last of the light.

Night cloaked the Iron Eagle in mist and moonlight. The wind screamed across the upper cliffs, and lanterns glowed like watchful eyes along the battlements. From their vantage point on a crag just above the stronghold, the group huddled behind a curtain of wind-scoured stone.

Ro lowered her spyglass again. "Shifts change every two hours. We'll have a window after midnight when the outer ramp is less guarded. That's our best chance."

"And your father?" Zavalla asked quietly.

Seth's jaw clenched. "If he's here, he's in the lower cells. Those look carved directly into the cliff beneath the eagle's talons. We'll have to go in quiet."

Milo looked at the frozen chasm below and let out a low whistle. "We'll also have to go in smart. That place is crawling with guards, and probably worse."

Zavalla added, "The Modo are powerful, but primitive. They distrust magic and avoid mystical items altogether. Their technology is crude, but brutal. If they've altered this place, it's with muscle and fire."

His hand rested briefly on the obsidian ring he wore—a treasure recovered from the lost island. Its surface, dark as the void, was etched with strange runes that pulsed faintly with a silvery-blue light. An iron eagle was set into the band itself, wings spread as if in flight. Zavalla had noticed this ring bore a striking resemblance to the giant Idol.

Ro narrowed her eyes. "Then we'll use that against them."

Zavalla held up a hand, and a whisper of violet light shimmered from his fingertips. "I'll mask our approach with a shadow veil. Not invisibility—but enough to bend the light. Stay close."

"We should move soon," Ro said. "The snow's falling harder. We can use the weather to our advantage."

The descent was treacherous. The path wound across narrow switchbacks, and snow packed against their boots made every step a risk. Ember stayed behind, tucked into a rock crevice to avoid notice. Milo gave her a scratch behind the horn and whispered, "Don't worry. We'll be back. With stories."

Under the cloak of shadow magic, they slipped past the outer towers and made their way toward the rear scaffolding—a rusted maintenance path once used by Nowin engineers.

The deeper they crept into the stronghold, the more the ancient iron of the structure groaned beneath them. Cracks lined the walls where the Modo had roughly patched sections with stone and timber. There were no signs of advanced mechanisms— only torch brackets, crude stone altars, and the scent of old blood. The fortress bore no signs of machinery—only the raw marks of a society that prized strength above all else. Reclaimed it as a place of strength through simplicity and fear. A prison. A lair. A shrine to raw power.

And tonight, it was a temple.

Below, in the grand chamber hollowed beneath the eagle's iron wings, the Modo were gathering. Dozens of them—hulking, wolf-like creatures with thick limbs and ragged fur—stood in a rough circle around a brazier filled with black flame. Their jaws protruded with sharp teeth, and their eyes gleamed with hunger and reverence. Around their necks hung necklaces made of teeth, some bearing dozens—each a mark of a victory, a kill, a conquest. The larger the necklace, the greater the warrior. They moved with brutish confidence, armed with crude steel and bone-forged axes. Their king, Modo himself, stood near the brazier, the largest of them all—his muscles thick as tree trunks and his hide marked with scars and ceremonial ash.

Chanting in deep guttural tones, they began a sacrifice—a ceremony to their idol, the Iron Eagle. They raised their weapons, howling to the metal ceiling as if calling for the great machine to awaken. Offerings of meat and bone were hurled into the fire.

And in a cage above the flame stood a defiant Nowin warrior— broad-shouldered, his crystal-inlaid armor scorched but intact, and his eyes blazing with fury. His white-furred arms were streaked with ash and dried blood, and one of his upper tusks was missing, torn clean from his jaw—the trophy of a Modo chieftain who had taken it in battle. This was no broken prisoner, but a proud warrior captured to be made a worthy sacrifice to the Iron Eagle. The Modo surrounded him with hungry eyes, eager to please their false god with the blood of one of their sworn enemies.

The group stiffened as they watched.

"He's Nowin," Ro whispered. "We have to help him."

"Not our mission," Zavalla muttered, but his tone lacked conviction.

"But he's one of Frizgorn's," Seth said firmly. "We help him."

Zavalla glanced at the brazier flame, then nodded slowly. "The Modo fear magic. We can use that."

He whispered a spell under his breath. Shadows deepened, flickering unnaturally across the walls. A gust of wind swept through the chamber, swirling the fire into a sudden green blaze. Ghostly images of horned spirits danced through the smoke. The Modo recoiled, snarling and retreating with wide eyes, muttering in fearful tones.

Ro and Milo raced forward while Zavalla maintained the illusion. They scaled the platform and wrenched the cage door open using a bar of broken iron. The Nowin warrior stepped out on his own, bloodied but still strong, his remaining tusk bared in a growl of defiance. His breath steamed in the cold air, but his eyes remained sharp and unflinching. "I am Gossett," he growled, his voice steady despite the pain. "Son of Gossett."

"There are others," he rasped. "Cells below. Warriors and scouts. Left to rot. You must help them too."

Seth and the others exchanged glances. Then they ran.

Together with the Nowin, they stormed the lower holding cells. The prisoners were malnourished, but many still had strength. The group freed them all, including several Nowins. As they moved deeper through the final row of cells, they nearly passed by a shadowed figure—a man curled in the far corner, skeletal, unmoving.

Zavalla paused. "Wait."

Seth turned. His eyes met the hollow figure's, and the world stopped. The face was gaunt, the body frail—but unmistakably his.

His father.

"Get them to safety," Seth ordered, breath tight.

He stepped into the gloom, heart pounding as realization gripped him.

"Father? I thought you were dead," Seth whispered, kneeling beside him.

Romos stirred weakly, his eyes blinking through exhaustion. "Seth... is that really you? By the Nine, you've grown. You look just like your mother."

Seth swallowed, emotions tightening his voice. "It's me. I'm here. We're getting you out of here."

Romos gave a faint nod, his hand gripping Seth's forearm. "I never stopped hoping. Even when hope stopped making sense."

The Nowin warrior—Gossett—stood guard near the cell door, watching with sharp eyes as Seth helped his father to his feet. "We must go."

Seth nodded. "Help me with him. We're getting out together."

But the Modo had regrouped. Horns sounded. A warband charged into the tunnels.

191

The group, now joined by a handful of freed Nowin warriors, retreated fast through the narrow halls—but were soon cornered at the Iron Eagle's massive steel flank. The ancient Iron idol loomed, silent and immovable.

Zavalla, panting, caught sight of something—a raised panel near the base. Inlaid into it was a shape: an eagle with wings unfurled, surrounded by runes.

He reached for his ring.

The runes glowed.

"It's a key," he breathed. "Of course it's a key."

He pressed the ring into the panel. The runes flared, and the ancient iron groaned.

A seam split in the side of the machine. With a grinding hiss, a hidden hatch opened.

"Inside!" Ro yelled.

They ushered the prisoners through as arrows clattered off the Iron Eagle's hull. Zavalla entered last, the hatch sealing just as the Modo reached them.

Inside, the air was cold and stale, filled with the scent of oil and rust. The metal corridor stretched ahead, curved and ribbed like the inside of a great beast. Milo glanced around, wide-eyed. "This... this isn't just a statue," he murmured. "It's like the Rusty Turtle. But bigger. Meaner."

Ro ran her hand along one of the walls, feeling the strange warmth in the metal. "This is a machine. A flying one. Just like the old world used to make."

Zavalla, still catching his breath, stared at the faintly glowing conduits that lit as they stepped forward. "It's a war machine. An ancient one. And if it still works..."

"We can fly out of here," Seth said.

Ro nodded. "If we can figure out how to start it."

Milo clapped his hands together. "Well then. Let's wake the bird."

Chapter 37

The Flight of the Iron Eagle

he interior of the Iron Eagle hummed with ancient
energy, as if stirred awake from centuries of silence. A low
thrum vibrated through the metal floor beneath their feet. The
walls, though worn by time, pulsed with veins of dim light. It
was alive—dormant, but not dead.

Zavalla pressed his palm to the nearest control panel. Runes
sparked to life under his fingertips, responding to the ring on
his hand. "This machine predates the dragon wars," he
murmured. "The craftsmanship... it's like nothing I've ever
seen."

"Can it fly?" Ro asked.

"That's what we're about to find out," Seth replied, helping
Romos sit gently against the curved wall. His father's breath
was shallow, but his color had improved slightly. Gossett stood
nearby, keeping watch over the corridor with a silent intensity.

Milo examined a glowing terminal. "Looks like it needs a
sequence to power up. I don't suppose anyone here speaks...
ancient eagle runes?"

"I've studied enough symbols to try," Zavalla said. "But we'll
have to move fast. If the Modo break through—"

A low clang echoed from beyond the hatch, as if answering his
fear. The Modo hadn't given up.

"Keep working," Ro said, unsheathing one of her enchanted daggers. It shimmered in her hand, the silver hawk motif catching the strange interior light. "We'll buy you time."

Zavalla muttered a spell and passed his hand over the control panel. Lines of light bloomed across the console, flowing outward like a river.

The Iron Eagle stirred.

Somewhere deep within its hollow chest, gears began to churn. Hydraulic limbs groaned as the ship shifted, wings flexing in slow, mechanical motion. Outside, snow and dust fell in sheets from the cliff as the metal beast shook itself awake.

"You've got to be kidding," Milo breathed. "We're flying this thing?"

Seth smiled faintly. "If it flies, it flies. We don't have another choice."

A grinding whir signaled a lift engaging near the back of the hall. The floor dropped beneath them slightly, then rose again, now glowing brighter.

Zavalla looked up. "It's responding to the ring. But I think it needs more. Some sort of final activation." Ro noticed a pattern in the controls. "Try this," she said, and quickly began pressing a sequence of buttons.

The ship came fully alive.

Outside, the Modo warriors had begun scaling the cliff, but the Iron Eagle shuddered, lifted—massive talons retracting from the cliffside. Jets of steam vented from its back. Fire sparked beneath its wings.

"Brace yourselves!" Zavalla shouted.

The Iron Eagle rose with a scream of metal and fire. Its engines roared, propelling them skyward in a thunderous blast of wind and heat.

Below, the stronghold erupted into chaos. The Modo scattered. Those too close were thrown back by the force of its ascent.

As the Iron Eagle climbed above the frozen peaks, the clouds parted. The sky opened wide before them.

And they flew.

Toward freedom. Toward the Nowin Kingdom.

As the Iron Eagle gained altitude, Zavalla adjusted controls, turning the vessel slightly in the sky. Below, the fortress loomed—dozens of Modo warriors scrambling in confusion. Milo found what looked like a targeting crystal and shouted, "I think this one fires something!"

Zavalla narrowed his eyes, recognized the spell-etched console, and activated it. The Iron Eagle responded with a series of thunderous pulses—lances of lightning erupted from beneath its wings, striking the fortress below. Towers crumbled. The idol flames were doused in a blaze of ancient fury.

The stronghold was devastated. The Modo scattered in every direction. What had once been their sacred seat of power was reduced to rubble and ash in moments.

Later, once the Iron Eagle had stabilized, Romos sat quietly beside Seth in the main corridor. From beneath his worn tunic, he pulled a carved wooden flute, etched with tiny dragon motifs.

"Your grandfather gave this to me," he said. "Said it could call a bonded dragon from anywhere in the world. The Modo let me keep it. They seemed to enjoy the music, oddly enough. If you're ever in danger and need your dragon, use it. Your dragon will come." He placed it gently in Seth's hand.

"Keep it close," he added. "It could save your life."

Seth took the flute and held it for a moment, feeling its weight, its warmth. Then he brought it to his lips and blew.

A clear, haunting note rang out through the chamber. The air vibrated.

From a side panel viewport, Seth watched the frozen landscape rush past.

"The Nowins will remember this," he said quietly. "We just changed the war."

In the distance, he saw a familiar glint of orange and gold—Ember, soaring through the sky, following them.

The ship banked south.

The ship banked south, returning to King Frizgorn's fortress with the rescued Nowin warriors. The Iron Eagle descended in awe-inspiring silence, settling onto a stone platform as the city turned out to greet them.

They had become heroes. And now, Romos could begin to heal.

The Iron Eagle groaned as it descended—its joints rattling, wings locking in place with a shriek of grinding metal. The landing was anything but graceful. The great machine wobbled as one of its rear talons clipped a stone outcropping, sending the vessel into a lurch. Milo yelped as he slammed into a bulkhead.

"Well," he muttered, rubbing his head, "we landed. More or less."

The ship shuddered one last time, then went still. Steam hissed from vents. Sparks popped from the walls. Whatever ancient power had stirred it to flight now seemed spent.

Ro peered down a flickering control panel. "I'm not sure she'll ever fly again."

Zavalla nodded grimly. "But she got us here. That's what mattered."

Chapter 38

The Hammer and the Highlands

he group returns to King Frizgorn's fortress as heroes, having destroyed the Modo stronghold and rescued numerous prisoners, including Romos Bergan. The Nowins celebrate their victory with a feast unlike any the group has seen—tables of roasted meats, glowing root dishes, and hearty stews served in carved crystal bowls. Milo grins, sampling the glowing root dish. "Nowin food—still undefeated," he said proudly, licking his fingers. "If we survive this quest, I might just retire here as a chef."

Seth is in good spirits for the first time in days, comforted by the presence of his father and the warmth of the company. Romos, though still weak from captivity, begins to regain strength thanks to rest and the continued support of the enchanted pot Milo had used to cook a restorative broth.

That night, Seth and Ro spend quiet moments together on a terrace overlooking the mountains. The stars hung like scattered embers overhead, and the cold air made their breath mist between quiet words. They stood side by side wrapped in borrowed furs, their shoulders just brushing, saying little at first.

"I used to look at the stars when I was little," Ro said quietly. "Made me feel like something else was out there... something more."

"You weren't alone," Seth replied. "Even if you felt like it."

She turned to him with a faint smile. "You always say the right thing. Even when you don't try."

"I try more than I let on." He smiled back, then added, "Only with you."

Their connection deepened—no longer just trust forged in battle, but something warmer, something real. Ro rested her head lightly against his shoulder, and Seth leaned into her, letting the silence say what neither of them quite dared to speak. They didn't say the words, not yet—but they didn't need to. It was clear in the closeness, in the way neither wanted the night to end.

The next morning, Seth met with his father again.
Romos, still unable to walk far, sat near a window facing the sunlit peaks.

Seth told him everything: the dragon treasures, the Shield of Compassion, the quest that lay ahead—and that his mother was one of the Nine Dragons of Existence.

Romos listened carefully, then let out a hoarse laugh. "A dragon, huh? I know," he said with a grin. "But that's a tale for another time." Then he clasped his son's shoulder. "Then you must go," he said. "But promise me you'll come back. I want to see Golden Arrow again... with you."

Seth promised.

In recognition of their honor and bravery, King Frizgorn presented the group with a legendary artifact: Glimmroth, a giant crystal-breaking warhammer forged in ancient times by Nowin artisans. The warhammer, known as Glimmroth, was said to have shattered the cursed tombs of the ancient frost kings. Its head was shaped like a chiselled block of jade-crystal, dense and resonant, with silver bands etched in old runes of shattering. The haft, wrapped in fur-lined leather, balanced the weight perfectly—making it as much a symbol of trust as it was a weapon of legend.

Frizgorn held it with reverence before offering it to Seth. "This hammer has broken cursed vaults and shattered enchanted fortresses. If the stories of Crystal Mountain are true, you'll need it. But understand—this is not a gift. It is a loan. Return it to me when your quest is done."

Seth accepted the weapon with a nod, testing its weight in his hand. "This would be the perfect weapon for a big guy like Milo," he added with a grin.

Milo looked up, mock offended. "Hey, I'll have you know I'm delicate and refined. Besides, I already carry the group's morale and meals—what more do you want?"

With gear packed, new fur-lined cloaks gifted by the Nowins, and a renewed sense of purpose, the group set their course toward the distant white peaks of Crystal Mountain. Snow gusted high along the horizon as the fortress faded behind them.

The next trial awaited—and it would be their hardest yet.

Chapter 39

The Road Through Frost

The wind bit with needle-like sharpness as the group departed from the safety of Frizgorn's fortress. Clad in heavy Nowin furs, they pressed into the blinding white expanse, the world around them reduced to swirling snow and shadowed shapes. Crystal Mountain remained hidden beyond the horizon —concealed by thick clouds and a veil of icy mist that clung stubbornly to the land.

Ember flew above in short bursts, vanishing and reappearing like a flicker of flame against the storm's white curtain. The snow drifts grew deeper, forcing the group to wade through the cold with each labored step. Ice-laced trees loomed like frozen giants, their branches groaning under the weight of snow.

"I swear this valley is uphill both ways," Milo grumbled, shifting the massive pack on his shoulders. "And if Ember doesn't spot a shortcut soon, I'm going to start digging us a tunnel."

Ro, her face half-hidden beneath her hood, snorted. "You wouldn't make it two feet without eating the snow."

Seth adjusted his grip on his walking stick and scanned the white void ahead. "If we're lucky, we'll make it to the first ridge by nightfall. But we won't see the mountain until we're right beneath it."

Zavalla rode in silence atop his summoned shadow-steed, his violet eye narrowed against the storm. "This storm isn't just weather. The mountain is masking itself. Something here doesn't want to be seen."

Then it happened.

A low *crack* echoed through the valley.

Ember screeched from above and banked sharply. The ground shivered. A distant roar—like the growl of the world itself—rose over the ridge.

"Avalanche!" Zavalla bellowed.

The sound grew—deafening, rumbling, alive. Snow began to shear off the cliffs above like a tidal wave of ice. Seth grabbed Ro's arm and yanked her toward a rocky outcropping as a wall of white descended.

"Move! Go—now!"

Zavalla raised one hand, and a ripple of shadow pulsed outward from his steed's hooves. Snow parted slightly around him as if avoiding his presence, his cloak billowing like smoke in the wind.

"Follow the shadows!" he barked, gesturing toward the narrow path he carved through the chaos.

But the path closed almost as fast as it formed. Ro and Seth scrambled forward, but Milo slipped—his heavy pack dragging him down into a sink of rushing snow.

From above, Ember dove like a streak of fire through the grey sky. She tucked her wings close, shot between craggy trees, and slammed into the snow where Milo had vanished. With

203

claws buried in his thick coat, she lifted him—grunting from the effort—and flapped furiously.

She couldn't carry him far—but it was enough.

Ember hauled Milo a few staggering feet through the air and dropped him behind the outcropping, where Seth caught and dragged him the rest of the way to safety. The avalanche thundered past moments later, swallowing the trail behind them.

They huddled under the rock, breathless and stunned.

Milo wheezed and blinked up at Ember, who panted beside him, wings twitching.

"Okay," he coughed, "remind me to give her *all* the spiced goat next time."

Ro knelt beside them, checking for injuries. "She's still not big enough to ride," she said, brushing snow from Ember's horns, "but I think she just proved size isn't everything."

Seth nodded, heart pounding. Ember looked back at him and gave a low, proud rumble.

Zavalla approached last, his steed stepping effortlessly atop the snowdrifts. His face was unreadable beneath his hood, but the violet glow in his eye dimmed as he took in the wreckage.

"That wasn't just nature," he murmured. "Something ancient is stirring."

That night, they found a jagged cliff to camp beneath. Ember curled close to the group, her warmth melting a ring in the snow. Milo stirred a stew in his copper pot, the magical heat humming gently in the silence.

Ro cracked a smile as Milo fussed with the pot, shielding it from the wind. "You'd think a fire-breather would be a better windbreak."

They laughed softly, but the joy was fleeting—quickly swallowed by the vast, eerie quiet of the frozen wilds.

Seth took the first watch, eyes scanning the black ridge above.

The avalanche had been a warning.

And something—some ancient force—was still watching.

Chapter 40

The Guardian

 y morning, the winds had stilled—but the silence that followed was even more unsettling.

The group broke camp beneath a brittle gray sky. Snow crunched beneath their boots like shattered glass, and every breath hung in the sharp air. Crystal Mountain remained shrouded in mist, but it loomed closer now—its immense white slopes rising like a god's shoulder beyond the valley.

By midday, they reached the mountain's outer edge.

The landscape changed abruptly. Trees gave way to jagged stone and ice-slick fields. The wind returned, whispering low across a graveyard of frozen history. Towering stone statues lined the trail—many cracked or toppled, their features long worn smooth by wind and time. Some bore swords. Others held shields or staves. Guardians, perhaps. Or warnings.

Scattered among them were remnants of past attempts to breach the mountain's secrets: shattered siege gear frozen in place, broken wheel axles tangled in drifts, and frost-coated remains of ancient camps half-buried in snow. Tents collapsed under ice. Tools rusted in skeletal hands. Banners hung in tatters from spears stuck like grave markers in the ground.

Ro crouched near a weather-beaten ridge where a half-buried banner flapped weakly in the wind. She brushed snow from the surface—then froze.

"It's from Zarnoth," she said, her voice tight. "The Swordsman Guild."

Seth moved to her side, eyes narrowing. "You're sure?"

Ro nodded and held up a broken emblem—silver and black, shaped like twin blades crossing over a hawk's wing.

"This camp was theirs—one of the expeditions sent before the kingdom gave up on Crystal Mountain."

Zavalla approached, staring at the broken gear and weathered ruins. "If the stories are true," he said slowly, "they didn't fail because of the cold."

Milo shifted uncomfortably. "You mean the guardian?"

Zavalla nodded. "A creature made of crystal and snow. Said to have six arms and eight wings—forged by the mountain to protect what lies within."

"The cave," Ro added. "At the mountain's base. That's where the gauntlets are hidden."

"And Lock," Seth said, remembering the tale told by the bard. "The green-armored warrior—trapped in the crystal. Still holding the treasure."

A tremor rolled beneath their feet—subtle, but unmistakable. Ember growled low and stepped in front of Milo, wings twitching.

From the mist ahead, something moved.

The group drew weapons, falling into a wide arc.

Then they saw it.

207

A towering figure, easily fifteen feet tall, stood half-encased in jagged crystal near the base of a narrow cliff. Six thick arms folded across its torso, and eight long, angular wings of cracked crystal curved behind its back like broken glass. Its face was smooth and featureless—an eerie, masklike blank.

Then one wing moved.

Seth raised his shield on instinct.

The creature's head turned slowly toward them, and the ice around its limbs groaned and fractured. A rumble echoed through the canyon like the grinding of stone.

"It's not guarding the treasure," Ro whispered. "It's guarding the *way in*."

The creature's feet shifted. Cracks spidered across the frozen ground as it took its first step forward—slow, deliberate, and thunderously heavy.

The mountain guardian had awoken.

The guardian took another step—then another.

Ice cracked and shattered beneath its immense weight. Its eight crystal wings spread wide, catching the grey light like jagged glass. Each of its six arms flexed with slow, deliberate menace. No eyes, no mouth—just a featureless mask and a presence that made the air grow heavier with every breath.

Seth raised his shield and stepped forward. "Hold position!"

Ro flanked left, blades drawn. Zavalla's staff pulsed faintly, and Milo—trembling—pulled his ladle from his belt and held it like a short club.

"Milo," Seth said, glancing over. "What are you doing? You're not seriously—"

"What does it look like? I'm gonna stir things up!" Milo said, raising the ladle like a weapon.

Seth didn't waste time arguing. He swung his pack around and pulled free a short-handled warhammer with a thick, square head engraved with angular script and spiral markings unique to Nowin craftsmanship. The leather grip was dark green and worn smooth from years of use.

"Here. Glimmroth," Seth said, pressing it into Milo's hands. "Frizgorn said it can break crystal from this mountain. It was forged from molten ore taken from its heart."

Milo blinked. "You're giving me *that* hammer?"

"You're the strongest one here. Just swing hard."

Milo clutched the hammer with both hands, nodding quickly. "Alright. But I'm still calling it *The Tenderizer* in my head."

The creature moved first.

It surged forward—faster than expected. The snow exploded beneath its feet as it swept a massive arm sideways. Seth braced with the Shield of Compassion, absorbing the brunt of the blow, but was hurled backward through a snowbank.

Ro darted in and slashed at its flank. Her blades scraped across the crystal body with a screech but left no mark. Zavalla hurled a bolt of violet fire that sparked against its chest—again, no damage.

209

Then Milo swung Glimmroth.

The hammer struck one of the guardian's lower arms with a thunderous crack. For a moment, something gave—a thin fracture spread across the point of impact, and a shard of crystal snapped free.

"Tenderized!" Milo shouted, eyes wide with equal parts triumph and panic.

Ro saw it. "It works!"

But the guardian didn't pause.

It twisted with unnatural speed, one of its upper arms sweeping around in a brutal arc. Milo barely had time to yelp before the strike caught him across the chest and sent him tumbling backward through the snow like a sack of flour.

He groaned, dazed but alive, Glimmroth still clutched in his hands.

"Okay," he wheezed, "that was *not* tender…"

The guardian surged again. Two arms lifted high, ready to crush them both.

Then Ember leapt—spitting fire and fury—and slammed into the creature's side. Her flames licked uselessly against the crystal, but the impact threw the guardian off its rhythm.

One of the wings struck her mid-air.

She yelped and crashed to the ground, wings crumpling, smoke curling from her nostrils as she went still in the snow.

"EMBER!" Milo shouted, scrambling toward her, half-crawling through the ice.

Seth staggered to his feet, bruised and reeling. "Fall back! Now!"

Zavalla unleashed a shockwave of shadow that staggered the creature. It bought them precious seconds—just enough for Ro and Milo to drag Ember toward the crystal cave at the base of Crystal Mountain.

The guardian followed, wings unfolding in fury—but the passage was too narrow. With a final, echoing roar of frustration, it halted just outside, pacing like a lion behind glass.

The group collapsed inside the hidden cave, gasping for breath. Ember's breathing was shallow but steady. Snow melted in a ring around her from her residual heat.

Milo dropped Glimmroth with a dull thud beside him and didn't let go of Ember's claw.

For now—they were safe.

Chapter 41

The Spark That Remains

he cave was cold, but it wasn't the kind of cold that bit the skin. It was quiet, heavy, and still—the cold of deep time, of a place that hadn't known warmth for centuries. The group sat in the dim blue glow of bioluminescent crystals lining the ceiling, their flickers reflecting off walls that shimmered like glass.

Ember lay curled on a patch of fur and cloaks, her breathing shallow. The jagged wound along her side still pulsed faintly with light. Milo hovered nearby, grinding herbs into paste with trembling fingers, his pot-helmet resting at his side.

"She's strong," he muttered, more to himself than anyone else. "Stronger than she looks. Dragon bones don't break easy, right?"

Zavalla didn't respond. He stood with his back to the group, staff planted firmly in the ground, staring at the winding tunnels ahead. The veins of green light running through the cave walls throbbed slowly, like the heartbeat of the mountain.

"She shouldn't have been in the fight," Milo finally said. "She's not ready."

Seth turned sharply. "None of us were ready."

Ro looked up from her spot beside Ember. "That thing—whatever it was—it wasn't just a creature. It wasn't just hunting us. It was defending its nest."

Zavalla's expression darkened. "The guardian. It doesn't wait—it protects. This mountain is its domain."

"I thought you said we could take it," Milo snapped. "You said we could handle this."

"I said we had to try," Zavalla growled. "Do you think I wanted this?"

Silence fell. Ember whimpered in her sleep, wings twitching.

Seth stood and crossed to the wall, placing a hand on a protruding crystal. "The Lopkin said, 'One breaks. One betrays.'" His voice was quiet, haunted. "Does this mean, Ember? Is she broken? Will she die?"

Ro stared at him, tears flickering in her eyes.

"No," Ro whispered. "Not yet."

Ro held up her amulet, its ruby core pulsing faintly. "The Amnathoth is glowing. It's guiding us deeper. The gauntlets are down there. They're supposed to heal, right?" She looked to Zavalla.

Zavalla gave a small nod. "If the legends are true." He knelt beside Ember and placed his hand gently above her wound, channeling a soft violet light from his palm. "My magic won't heal this… but it can dull the pain. I can keep her comfortable—alive—until you return."

Milo adjusted the straps on his pack, his jaw clenched and eyes hard with fury. "I'm going after the Rockworms," he snapped.

"That thing hurt Ember—and I know Rockworm acid will hurt it back. When you're done with the knight, I want that hammer back. I've got some tenderizing to do."

He tugged the pack tighter, pulling out the vials Frizgorn gave them—reinforced with crystal lattice. "If we're lucky, these'll hold the acid without melting."

Seth reached for the hammer on Milo's belt. "Glimmroth. I'll need this." Milo handed it over, reluctantly, his fingers lingering on the grip before letting go.

Ro nodded to Seth. "Come with me. The amulet's pull is stronger now. We're close."

Seth followed her into the deepening tunnels, leaving Zavalla and Ember behind.

Guided by the glowing pulse of Ro's amulet, they descended until the cave opened into a hollow chamber. The crystals spiraled along the walls, forming arcs of emerald and glass. At the center, a massive crystal shell was fused to the rock—inside it, unmoving, stood a warrior clad in green armor, his body half-turned as if frozen mid-lunge.

His eyes were shut. His arms locked forward, hands clenched around an invisible weapon.

Seth stepped forward, raising Glimmroth.

"This is what it was made for," he said. "Stand back."

With a breath and a whispered word, he brought the hammer down.

214

Cracks webbed across the shell. A second strike. Then a third.

The crystal shattered.

A gasp tore from the warrior's throat as he stumbled forward, falling to his knees. Ro rushed to support him.

His eyes fluttered open—glowing faint green. He looked at her, then at the others. "Where... am I?"

"You're safe now," Ro whispered. "You're among friends."

The knight steadied himself, rising to his feet. His armor clanked—heavy and ancient—and a horned green helm shaded most of his face, but his glowing green eyes were clearly visible beneath it. As he stood, Seth and Ro exchanged surprised glances.

"He's... a Dwarve?" Ro whispered.

"Thought he would be taller," Seth murmured back.

"My name... is Lock," the knight said, voice low and steady.

"Last I remember I was in the Dark Forest and a large glowing beast came at me from the sky." He blinked slowly, then looked down at his empty hands. "Where is my saber?" he said with urgency, his eyes scanning wildly. "I need it. I swore an oath to my father—to keep the Dark Forest free of nightmares, to make it safe for travelers. I can't fulfill that without my blade."

He looked at Seth, then Ro.

"We need your help," Ro said, her voice firm. "A friend of ours is wounded—badly. We came here hoping to find the Gauntlets of Verdance. They're said to heal anything."

215

Lock's green eyes narrowed, then softened. He raised his hands. "The Gauntlets… you mean these?"

Seth stepped forward. "Will you use them?"

Lock nodded slowly. "Lead the way. Let's get back to your friend."

They moved quickly, retracing their steps through the shimmering tunnels. The amulet's glow guided them surely, lighting the path like a heartbeat pulsing in the dark. Neither Seth nor Ro spoke much—each step carried the weight of hope and desperation.

When they emerged into the cavern where Ember lay, Milo looked up, tense and expectant. Zavalla knelt beside her, exhausted and pale, his head bowed low. He didn't speak. His hands hovered just above Ember's side, the faint glow of his magic flickering—then fading.

For a moment, no one breathed.

"She's too still," Ro whispered.

Zavalla shook his head slowly, regret in his eyes.

But Lock stepped past them all. "If there is still a spark.," he said firmly.

His armor clanked softly with each step.

Lock stepped forward, placing his gauntleted hand on Ember's side. The green glow from his palm spread across her wound. Ember stirred, eyes blinking open. The light pulsed, then faded —not leaving even a thin scar.

Milo gasped. "She's... she's healed."

He dropped to his knees beside her, laughing through the tears welling in his eyes. "You fire-hearted rascal. You scared me half to death."

Ro knelt on Ember's other side, brushing a hand gently along the newly healed scales. "I thought we lost her," she breathed.

Ember gave a soft rumble, stretching her wings just slightly as her amber eyes blinked open fully.

Seth let out a shaky breath he hadn't realized he was holding. "She's really back."

Even Zavalla managed a faint smile.

For a few heartbeats, joy warmed the cold cavern.

Ro looked at Lock, then back at the others. "We have what we came for. Now let's finish what we started."

As the group gathered themselves, Zavalla remained still, his gaze fixed on the glowing gauntlets now resting at Lock's sides. His expression was unreadable, but his eyes burned with longing.

He had seen them in visions, read of their power in the lost tomes of Loopkin. To heal—not just others, but himself. The pain in his legs, the damage left by the PAW, the weight he had carried for years—could it finally end?

Zavalla's voice was quiet. "Those gauntlets... they could heal more than wounds."

Lock looked at him but said nothing.

Seth turned, noticing the shift in Zavalla's expression.

217

But the moment passed. Zavalla lowered his gaze and turned away, his staff tapping softly against the stone floor.

Chapter 42

The Guardian Falls

he mood in the cavern had shifted. Ember's recovery

had lit a new fire in them all—hope, fierce and unyielding. They could win. They *would* win.

Milo wiped his eyes with the edge of his sleeve and stood, his pot-helmet clanging slightly as he set it atop his head. "Right then," he said with a grin, "I believe I owe that oversized crystal freak a spicy serving of Rockworm vengeance."

Lock tightened the straps on his armor. "We strike together this time. With purpose."

Seth nodded. "We draw it out. Keep it moving. Ro, you and I flank it."

He turned to Milo and handed Glimmroth back. "You'll need this more than I will."

Milo grinned, gripping the hammer with satisfaction. "That's more like it."

Then he reached into his pack and pulled out a set of small glowing vials. "Here—take the acid," he said, handing one to Ro. "You're quicker. Get close and throw it when the beast opens a gap."

"I'll keep its attention," Lock said. "My armor is enchanted—it makes me immortal. And with the Gauntlets of Verdance, even if I'm injured, I'll heal right away." He looked at each of them with calm certainty. "I'm your secret weapon."

Zavalla tapped the ground with his staff, eyes sharp. "And I'll trap its footing with magic when I can."

Their plan was hastily drawn but clear. They left the cave behind and returned to the place of their earlier failure, this time with hardened resolve.

The guardian was waiting—tall and imposing, its crystalline body gleaming with jagged edges and radiant fractures. It stood nearly fifteen feet high, shimmering with the energy of the mountain itself. The entire canyon felt like an extension of its being, as if the terrain had shaped itself around the creature's will. It shrieked when it saw them.

This time, they did not hesitate.

The battle was brutal, each strike echoing like thunder through the caves.

The guardian towered over them, its six crystal arms spinning and lashing like blades, each movement sending dazzling reflections across the cavern. Its eight crystalline wings pulsed with raw energy, creating sudden bursts of wind and cutting shards of light.

Lock charged first, drawing the guardian's full fury. Its claws slashed and struck, but though his enchanted armor could not be damaged, each blow that struck his body was swiftly healed by the Gauntlets of Verdance. He pressed forward without faltering, a glowing green force of will, keeping the beast focused on him.

Ro and Seth moved in sync, weaving around the creature's limbs, striking and retreating before its wings could sweep them aside. Ro scaled a ledge and hurled the vial of Rockworm acid onto one of its legs. The liquid hissed and steamed, eating away at the crystal like fire on ice.

The guardian shrieked, a piercing, echoing wail that shook dust loose from the cavern ceiling. It reared back and slammed two of its arms into the ground, sending shockwaves through the floor. Seth barely leapt aside in time.

Zavalla raised his staff, channeling deep into the cavern's magic. "Bind it!" he shouted. Runes flared beneath the guardian's feet as chains of violet light burst forth, coiling around its legs and dragging it down.

"Again!" Ro yelled.

Milo dashed in, gripping Glimmroth—'the Tenderizer,' as he proudly called it—with both hands. For once, there were no jokes on his lips, just a grim determination that made him almost unrecognizable.

"Time to tenderize," he muttered, low and gravelly, swinging the hammer into a fractured section of the guardian's torso.

The impact boomed. "Medium rare!" he grunted, breath ragged.

Cracks splintered across the guardian's chest, but it retaliated, swiping a massive claw that slammed into Milo and sent him skidding across the stone.

He groaned, pushing himself up, blood at the corner of his mouth. "Still standing," he growled. "That was just the marinade."

Lock leapt forward once more, absorbing a blow across the shoulder before plunging his sword arm into the creature's central chest crystal, holding it in place.

"Now!" Zavalla cried.

Milo ran, raised Glimmroth, and with a final yell, slammed the hammer into the weakened spot.

"Finish your dessert!" he snarled through gritted teeth. "Looks like dinner's served—this one's cooked to perfection!"

With a groaning, shuddering crack, the guardian finally collapsed—its body fracturing into a thousand glittering shards that scattered across the cavern floor.

Silence returned.

In the rubble, something glimmered—an old hilt, emerald-set and pulsing faintly. Lock stepped forward, reverent, and lifted the blade from beneath the broken crystal plates.

"My saber," he whispered.

He turned to the group, gratitude in his eyes. "You freed me, healed me, and helped me reclaim this. I owe you more than words."

The tension from the battle eased as the group finally had a chance to catch their breath. Sitting among the glittering remains of the guardian, they shared their stories. Ro spoke of the treasures, of the quest that had brought them across seas and through ruins. Milo chimed in with quiet pride about their narrow escapes—and their meals. Zavalla, more reserved, spoke of the ancient magics stirring again in the land. Seth spoke last, sharing their purpose with a quiet conviction.

Lock listened carefully. "You seek the Nine Treasures of the Dragons of Existence," he said at last. "Then we walk paths not so different." He looked at his saber, running a hand along the edge. "I swore to keep the Dark Forest free of nightmares. This blade and I have a duty. And thanks to you, I can fulfill it once more."

He glanced down at his saber, thoughtful. "This blade once belonged to me—as the Green Armored Knight. Some say I wasn't human, but a being of spiritual power. Each night, I rode a majestic black horse through the Dark Forest, battling summoned demons and creatures of nightmares, all while tracking a black-cloaked figure who spread fear across the land. I did it to protect the city of Elsdone—and to banish the nightmares from our reality.

After every battle, I would dismount, kneel beside my fallen foes, and chant ancient words while pointing the saber at their bodies. A dark green glow would envelop them—and then, they would vanish. Even I never fully understood why. It was a calling. A ritual. A duty."

Lock's voice lowered. "On the night of Elson the 16th, as I performed the ritual once more, a huge white, glowing creature with eight wings descended upon me. It spoke the same strange words… and you know the rest of that story."

Lock gave a slow nod. "Perhaps. My father and I, a wizard named Larcan… together, we ran Larcan & Lock's Magic Shop in a Box. Larcan was a great enchanter, and I was the blacksmith. We'd appear in towns with only a trunk. Open it, and stairs would lead down into a full magical shop. That life ended when he was struck down in the Dark Forest on a journey to Elsdone."

He looked to the cave's shimmering light above. "After Larcan died in the Dark Forest, I took up the green armor and began riding through the forest at night, hunting the same creatures that killed him—and keeping the roads safe for travelers. Some say I did it to honor him—others say it was vengeance. He was my adopted father. I carry both our legacies now—and I intend to finish what we started."

Ro's eyes narrowed thoughtfully. "That black-cloaked figure you spoke of… what if he has the Cloak of Nightmares? It would explain everything we've heard. If so, it's waiting for us in the Dark Forest."

Lock nodded. "Then our paths will cross again. You'll find me there when the time comes."

He turned to Seth and gently removed the Gauntlets of Verdance from his arms, offering them without hesitation. "These belong with you now. Without you, I'd still be frozen in time."

Seth accepted them with quiet awe.

As the group made their way back toward the mountain pass that led to King Frizgorn's castle, the weight of the fight gave way to something greater.

They were more than survivors now.

They were beginning to feel like heroes.

<h1 style="text-align:center">Chapter 43</h1>

<h1 style="text-align:center">Return to Frizgorn's Castle</h1>

Before the group could fully disperse, Seth stepped toward Zavalla and slowly removed the Gauntlets of Verdance from his arms. "You should take these," he said. "You've carried us with your magic. You're the one who understands the balance we're dealing with better than any of us."

Zavalla hesitated, then nodded solemnly as he accepted the gauntlets. As the magic of the artifact wrapped around him, a glow shimmered across his limbs. The stiffness in his posture melted away.

He straightened fully—taller, stronger. His cane slipped from his grip and clattered to the floor.

"I can feel it," he murmured, eyes wide. "My natural power… it flows again. I haven't felt this since I was young—before I was crippled."

He stood with renewed presence, the old weight in his voice steadied by strength. The group watched in quiet amazement, none daring to interrupt.

Seth then turned to Ember, removing the Aquarian Crown from his satchel. He gently placed it on her head, the seafoam circlet fitting just behind her horns. "If anything happens to us, you run," he whispered. "Carry it to safety. You're faster than any of us."

Ember chirped softly in response, her eyes gleaming.

The climb down Crystal Mountain was steep, but the mood among the group had shifted. Where once there had been tension and exhaustion, now there was unity—an unspoken bond forged in battle, sealed in the glow of Ember's healing, and strengthened by the knowledge that they had saved not just a life, but a legacy.

As the icy wind howled through the mountain pass, Seth walked near the front, cloak wrapped tightly around his arms.

"Think Frizgorn will believe us when we tell him we shattered a crystal monster and woke up a myth?" Milo asked, trying to keep pace while balancing his pot-helmet and pack.

"He'd better," Ro said, flashing a tired grin. "We've got bruises and one grumpy dragon to prove it."

Ember gave a soft snort and bumped against Ro's side, her wings flicking briefly in the wind.

By the time the snow thinned and the towers of Frizgorn's Castle came into view, the sun was beginning to dip, casting long amber shadows over the stone road. Guards at the outer wall spotted them quickly. One called out as the gates creaked open.

"Is that… them?"

"It's the ones the king sent South!" another cried. "They've returned!"

The castle's great hall buzzed with curiosity and quiet anticipation as the group was ushered inside. King Frizgorn waited atop his modest stone dais, his expression unreadable until he saw the gauntlets gleaming on Zavalla's arms.

"You found them," the king said simply.

"We did," Zavalla replied. "But not alone."

Seth recounted the story—of the guardian, of Lock, of the cave beneath the mountain. Ro added the details of the battle, and Zavalla, with his usual dry edge, explained the significance of the gauntlets and their connection to the Nine Treasures.

Frizgorn remained quiet for a long moment. Then he stepped down and approached Seth.

Frizgorn's gaze moved to the hammer in Milo's grip. "So Glimmroth served you well?"

Milo gave a proud nod. "It did more than that. It *cooked* a monster."

Frizgorn chuckled. "Then let it continue to serve. You've earned it. Keep it—and with it, the respect of our kingdom."

He looked across the group. "From this day forward, you are honored as Nowin heroes. You may travel freely throughout our kingdom. And you may pass through the Pass of Lost Knights without question."

Zavalla raised an eyebrow. "The Fergo Pass?"

Frizgorn nodded gravely. "That's what they call it now. The old name still stands for us—the Pass of Lost Knights. It lies in the northern range of the Snow-Capped Mountains. Ancient statues of knights line both sides of the path, all the way to the Fergo's side of Acklelend. For centuries, none who entered returned. The Fergo feared the statues, never daring to cross—until the War of the Mountains."

Ro crossed her arms. "So it's watched?"

"Always," Frizgorn said. "By both sides. But it remains the safest and most direct route through the range. If anyone questions your right to pass, just show them the hammer—it will speak for you."

He clapped a firm hand on Seth's shoulder, then turned to the others. "Rest here tonight. In the morning, we'll feast in your honor. After that… wherever your road takes you next, you'll leave with our blessing."

As they turned to go, Frizgorn called out again. "If you're heading to the Dark Forest, there's a path few know of—a secret trail that bypasses Devil's Falls entirely. It'll bring you just outside the forest, near a place called Enchanted Rock…"

"Enchanted Rock?" Ro echoed.

Frizgorn smiled faintly. "A massive stone resting in a small hollow north of the forest. Lovers often picnic there or rest beneath its shade. Some say it fell from the sky in a streak of light, crashing to earth in that very spot. And legend has it—if you kiss your true love upon the rock, nothing can ever part you."

Milo raised an eyebrow. "Romantic *and* useful."

Frizgorn nodded. "Take the hidden trail behind the east watchtower."

Later, just as the group was preparing to leave Frizgorn's Castle, Seth found his father seated by one of the carved crystal windows, warm light casting gentle patterns across the elder Bergan's worn face. He still looked thin, weathered from years of captivity, but there was more color in his skin, more strength behind his eyes.

Zavalla stood nearby, the Gauntlets of Verdance still glowing faintly on his arms.

"Are you ready?" Seth asked, kneeling beside his father.

Romos gave a tired but genuine smile. "I am. Though I won't be traveling with you this time."

Seth's brow furrowed. "What do you mean?"

Romos glanced at Zavalla, who stepped forward and placed a hand gently on the old man's shoulder. A warm, green light passed from the gauntlets into Romos's body. His posture straightened, his breathing deepened. The hollowness in his cheeks faded.

"It's time I return to Golden Arrow," Romos said, placing a firm hand on Seth's shoulder. "King Frizgorn is sending a group of Nowins to help escort me home. The village needs someone to tell them what really happened. And you—" He squeezed his son's shoulder. "You've got a world to save."

Seth swallowed hard, fighting back emotion. "You're really going back?"

Romos nodded. "And I'll be waiting for you there. When all this madness is done."

He paused, then added in a quieter voice, "I'm proud of you, Seth. More than words can say. I thought I'd never see you again, and now... look at you. You've become everything I hoped for and more."

229

They embraced, father and son. Not as they were, but as they had become—changed by time, pain, and the choices that defined them.

As the group gathered at the castle gates, Seth looked back one last time. Romos stood with the Nowins, wind catching the edge of his travel cloak, his chin lifted toward the northern mountains.

"Goodbye, Father," Seth whispered.

Then he turned, rejoining his friends. The road ahead waited, treacherous and long—but for the first time in ages, his heart carried more than duty.

It carried hope.

Far from Frizgorn's Castle, beneath the amber light of a setting sun, a cloaked figure hunched over a flickering lantern in the corner of a grimy tavern. Jackom Halfdill tapped his fingers on the warped wooden table, eyes darting toward the door.

Jackom leaned back in his chair, a crooked smile forming beneath his hood. A soft scratching drew his gaze to a shadowed perch above the hearth, where a small creature the size of a cat sat curled—a Mockin.

Its glossy eyes blinked with eerie intelligence, its form flickering as it shifted from a catlike silhouette to a black-feathered bird, then into the likeness of a mouse with Jackom's own smirk. Mockins were rare shapeshifters—able to mimic any small creature and repeat exactly what they heard, though always in a mocking, twisted tone.

Jackom chuckled. "Did you get everything?"

"Did you get everything?" the Mockin said back in a dimwitted voice, mimicking him with perfect mockery.

The Mockin then repeated Frizgorn's voice in a perfectly mocking tone: *"If you're heading to the Dark Forest, there's a path few know of—a secret trail that bypasses Devil's Falls entirely. It will take you just outside the forest to a place called Enchanted Rock..."*

"No one ever suspects the rat in the rafters," Jackom muttered, glancing at the shapeshifter with satisfaction. "You've outdone yourself."

"You've outdone yourself," the Mockin echoed, its tone laced with mocking delight.

A thin messenger stood nearby, nervously watching as Jackom sealed a scroll with black wax.

"To Marduk of Mar," Jackom muttered. "Tell him I have information. A bounty worth claiming. He'll want to hear what I know..."

The messenger nodded and vanished into the crowd, scroll in hand.

Then the Mockin, with a crooked grin, echoed Jackom's voice: *"Carry it safely!"*

Jackom grinned wider. "Good. Let's keep listening. I want Marduk to hear *everything*."

Chapter 44

The Shatter at Enchanted Rock

he stars above Enchanted Rock shimmered like frost

on glass, casting a silvery glow over the peaceful clearing. A soft breeze danced through the stonewood trees, and the legendary rock itself pulsed faintly with residual warmth from the day's sunlight. The group had made camp just north of the Dark Forest—high spirits settling over them like a blanket.

For once, there was no pressing danger. No riddles to solve, no monsters lurking. Only the quiet comfort of a moment hard-earned.

Milo stirred a pot over the fire, humming a tune that Ember seemed to mimic with soft purring chirps. Zavalla sat cross-legged near the edge of camp, eyes closed in meditation, the Gauntlets of Verdance glowing softly against his arms. He was stronger now—straighter. The burden of his pain had lifted.

Seth and Ro had wandered just out of sight, their footsteps quiet in the grass as they approached the smooth curve of Enchanted Rock. The moon cast their shadows long and intertwined.

"I used to think this was all myth," Ro whispered, brushing her fingers along the warm stone. "The rock, the prophecy, the treasures…"

Seth smiled, his hand finding hers. "And now?"

"I think I've never been more certain of anything in my life."

They leaned against the rock in silence, letting the world fall away.

Ro turned to him, her voice barely a whisper. "You're not what I expected to find when I first left Zarnoth."

Seth smiled gently. "You're still trying to steal from me."

Ro raised an eyebrow. "Oh?"

He touched his chest softly with two fingers, just over his heart. "That."

Ro's breath caught, and she stepped closer. "Maybe I'm not done yet."

She kissed him. It was soft and real, a moment born from everything they had survived together.

When they finally pulled apart, Seth rested his forehead against hers. "I don't think I'd stop you."

But silence would not last.

The attack came with fire.

Explosions burst through the trees, scattering embers and breaking branches as mercenaries in black and gold surged into the camp. Milo yelled a warning. Ember roared and launched into the air, fire spewing in defensive arcs. Zavalla rose to his feet instantly, calling forth a shield of violet light as crossbow bolts rained down.

From the shadows emerged Jackom Halfdill, smug and smiling, followed by soldiers bearing the seal of Mar. Behind them—tall, cruel, and armored in obsidian—came Marduk.

"Looking for a runaway?" Jackom called. "I've found your prize."

Ro reached for her daggers, but before she could move, a pair of anti-magic nets launched from the shadows and tangled around her. The enchantments within them flared to life, crackling as they suppressed her abilities. PAW agents never cast spells themselves—but they had no qualms using magic items when it served their agenda. The weight of the nets drove her to her knees.

Seth lunged, only to be struck in the side by a blunt, rune-inscribed baton wielded by one of the PAW enforcers. The blow knocked the wind from him and sent him sprawling to the ground, gasping before darkness overtook him.

"Enough," Marduke growled. "The princess of Zarnoth belongs to Mar now."

Ro gasped as the soldiers dragged her toward the carriages. "Don't hurt him!" she cried, but Seth was already unconscious —bound in runes and dragged toward a separate cage.

Zavalla threw spells like wildfire, holding off the advancing mercenaries, but there were too many. PAW agents surged forward, casting anti-magic nets that crackled with arcane suppression. One landed across Zavalla's shoulders, nearly bringing him to his knees.

"You cowards!" he roared, eyes blazing. "You claim to hate magic and now you use it against us? Hypocrites!"

Another net flew toward him—he blasted it mid-air with raw force, then raised both arms, summoning a violent surge of elemental energy. A jagged arc of violet lightning erupted from his fingertips, vaporizing two PAW agents in an instant. Their screams were cut short as their bodies were reduced to ash, scattered by the force of the spell.

Jackom turned to flee, but Zavalla's eyes locked on him.

"You won't slither away."

With a snarl, Zavalla thrust his staff forward. A shockwave of raw arcane power surged out, engulfing Jackom in a blinding blast. Jackom screamed as he was hurled back, his cloak in tatters, his body shattered and flung into the underbrush. When the smoke cleared, his body lay crumpled beside a scorched stump—his chest torn open, one arm missing, eyes glassed over in a final frozen expression of terror. The earth beneath him smoked and sizzled, his blood seared into the dirt. He would not rise again.

Fury drove Zavalla through the pain.

Meanwhile, Milo saw Seth's shield lying near the campfire— abandoned in the rush. He dashed over and grabbed it, slinging it across his back just as Ember—now the size of a small pony —rushed between his legs.

She crouched low, growling. Milo grunted and grabbed onto her back. She staggered for a moment under his weight, wings flaring for balance, then leapt into the night with a burst of

desperate strength. "What are you doing?! We have to turn back!" Milo yelled.

Together, they vanished into the woods.

Zavalla turned one last time, locking eyes with Marduk—and then with the PAW agents closing in on him.

"Come for me," he hissed, vanishing into a blast of smoke.

The firelight flickered.

The camp was shattered.

The group—broken.